The University of Penns, ...a

Caren Beilin

2013 NOEMI PRESS FICTION PRIZE WINNER

NOEMI PRESS

Noemi Press

P.O. Box 1330
Mesilla Park, NM 88047

www.noemipress.org

Library of Congress Cataloging-in-Publication Data

Beilin, Caren.
  [Short stories. Selections]
  The University of Pennsylvania / by Caren Beilin.
     pages cm
  ISBN 978-1-934819-37-1 (alk. paper) -- ISBN 1-934819-37-9 (alk. paper)
  1. University of Pennsylvania--Fiction. 2. Universities and colleges--Fiction. I. Title.
  PS3602.E384A6 2014
  813'.6--dc23
                              2014024064

Cover and interior design by Jana Vukovic: http//www.janavukovic.com

For my mother, Debbie Kooperman, and sister, Lauren Beilin.

Fall

Olivia is known by her affliction of continuous menstruation. She is said to have originated in Bethlehem, and is known also as the official heir to the Knox factory therein. But here, she attends the University of Pennsylvania, a freshman. The figure of Olivia, bleeding, as described by the ancients, has a beautiful face, delicate and terraqueous, and a nimble red uterus, binarious, in her bleeding—continuous.

She was once a trembling adolescent in her yard prone to moon-worshipping. She was not close with anyone, not even the Knoxes.

At the University of Pennsylvania, in Philadelphia, Olivia Knox lies on her slim dorm room bed, and worries—over having to share the large bathroom down the hall. In Bethlehem, she'd had an entire bathroom to herself, and this bathroom a lock and a large tub, too, where she could bleed forever if needed into the all-accepting drain. There is a drain's holy acceptance.

She cried out for her mother when the bleeding began. Fourteen. Sunday. She ran from the factory where she was helping her father, past his Benz and toward their mansion, up to the bedroom, her pants brown and clinging, and the two of them—mother, daughter— had been for hours unable to stop the bleeding. Helped to climb over a kitchen mitt, Olivia, bleeding, was driven down to Philadelphia, and there a doctor had to remove the mitt. He lowered the sopping girl over a basin, where then stomach lubricant was applied, and this doctor, unforgivably a man, would not even look at her but watched a screen with the black and white abomination of her binarious uterus wincing and bouncing in reaction to being seen—the *two* of them—*at last*. They did not look very real. They looked like Iceland.

On the drive down, looking out the Benz window, Olivia saw a cloud had turned dense outside, and she felt the moon was a prisoner above it. To see the moon is its freedom!

The doctor told her mother of her having two wombs and these beginning to bleed. Simultaneous. Mrs. Knox told her daughter—

"You are a woman now."

Inaccurate and apparent!

There was nothing that could be done about the blood, the doctor said. They had fit her into a diaper, ordered from the Obstetrics aisle of the hospital at the University of Pennsylvania. It was midnight by the time they could leave—Mrs. Knox slumped, her sickness now oozing out, effuse, alien person outside of pajama, too far off the map of her bedroom—and it rained wetting the roads as Olivia's blood filled the diaper, which fit fine, a good fit, over how slim her form, fourteen, and then it was on their Benz's immaculate leather, all over, and God bless the moon, Olivia now thought, looking right at it again, beyond this everything, perfection.

"We'll get you some tampons," Mrs. Knox said at last.

Olivia looked up at her moon, and imagined it killed, and she, a Lenape Indian, indigenous to this region—she would have to hunt it apart, to use all of its parts, my whitebison, its skin, bone and organ, I would dissect into everything! I will use the moon, slain and kissed with my iris, to find padding, to line my underwear with the shaved tufts of whitehotrock, that heightrock, until I reach into my deadmoon deeper and, Pennsylvanian, use tampons.

They were parked outside of a desolate WaWa, the asphalt a moonbutterous blackbread. There were no stars. Her mother was too tired to go in, had been too frail for any of this. And Olivia could not bear to go in alone.

The thought of going in alone . . . the dripping diaper puffed inside her pants . . . bloodsoiled shoes somehow . . . she could not. She'd rather make her bed that night in the tub. The pipes, wherever they let out . . . the ground would understand, understood blood in Bethlehem. You can't buy pad or tampon at night, a fourteen year old alone wearing a diaper, a Benz panting for you outside, its leather moistened and ruined. Everyone knew you. You were Olivia, bleeding, Knox.

"Just drive," Olivia told her mother, and Mrs. Knox—who was usually too frail, sick, and tired, to drive, or love—drove.

Olivia had been beginning to read everything. A good book is a pamphlet on how to leave your parents. A great book is longer and tells you how to leave your town. A very long book helps you with the waiting you are enduring. You are waiting for your father to die. You can't kill him. You don't shoot him. You are waiting for him to fall down, to clear the fat off the ceiling.

That is your particular patience, but in the meantime you are scrupulous about your application materials. You are applying to the University of Pennsylvania to study English therein, in the fall. To live in a dorm. You imagine your life. But you cannot yet move. You wait. Crouched. Hunched in the kitchen cabinet behind the buckets of your father's product—Knox Gelatin—the yield of his factory's motions, murder's powder. You want *irreconcilability itself* to part so you can leave the land, leave land. You read Sophocles. For an entire year, your junior, you only read plays. Shakespeare. You've read everything, so that you know. Everything. The king dies. He has to go!

By the time Olivia has entered college as an English major at the University of Pennsylvania, she is accustomed to using three or four tampons at a time. She changes them out frequently, as often as twice every hour. Seminars are a problem, as are long, mandatory group afternoons where a teaching assistant takes them to a room in the library and goes over the plots to several books at once, mostly British. The freshmen have to graph what happens, and all the while her tampons soaking, bulging with robinbreasts of blood, gore swirling onto her chair, and she cannot get her plots straight, or truly understand the language of irony, how iron might ping against what happens causing fractures, cleavage in which criticism is meant to seethe, all that happens confused with what is happening, the plots soaked in new blood, the marriages and quarrels and conflicts and wars mixing in her mind with the panic of utter embarrassment.

The large bathroom down the dorm hall at the University of Pennsylvania is so public. Girls gossip about their defecations side by side. Olivia sits inside a stall. Blood tumbles out of her, nauseating her still to look down when finished. She cannot get used to the sight. She has to flush and re-flush, until the water is not even pale with color, and then carefully pack tampon after tampon back in, four of them at once, and this for only the first half of her evening. She is always up after midnight. She tries incredibly hard, sometimes to the plight of sheets, to do without a diaper.

The nights are hardest. Impossible to sleep straight through without ruining everything, yes the sheets, and the dormnarrow mattress, down, she thinks, to the stones of this foundation—she thinks she can smell iron everywhere and assumes she is the culprit. She is filling the University of Pennsylvania full of blood, she thinks—filling its cracks, its pipes, and soon enough the faucets will speak her problem, the lecture halls and library groups will lift up on a sea of welling, now bursting, *murderwater*. Only a matter of time.

Olivia makes not one friend during her first weeks at the University of Pennsylvania, too busy with her bloody uterine stars, ever blinkering blood on the bed. It is not just blood! It is full of marbles and beans, something thick enough to be black, sometimes sick enough to be brown, sometimes wild, almost violet again. She weighs less than ninety pounds but her inner vagina expands vastly to accommodate the tampons. Huddling, waiting, filling, their tails like the talit she can see hanging from the shirts of the orthodox students here, who need their rooms on the first floor so as not to take the elevators on Sabbath Saturday. Olivia lives on this floor, too, in one of the larger dorm rooms alone, because of who she is, after all, a Knox, a name about as strong as a Penn, a wing of the hospital at the University of Pennsylvania named for her father even, Heathen!, though no one is allowed to realize this. She revels in being anonymous, not Olivia, bleeding, Knox.

Her neighbors are Adele and Beth. They are nineteen and eighteen. She thinks of them more as the Amish, with long skirts, and more, the same look, a pale, uneven face, the face of worth being elsewhere—not looked at in front—and here they are on the first floor close enough to earth, how the Amish have to be, too, kneeling, knees hanging with grass, these girls kneeling down on their thin dorm carpet facing east, which in the case of Adele and Beth means facing the hall, Olivia's dorm room door. She needs a forced intimacy, the intimacy of needing something simple. She could go ask for an egg.

For a book.

"Do you have a copy of *The Rainbow*? I need to read it by early tomorrow!" She tries the sound of ultra-concern, the way students at the University of Pennsylvania always sound about what needs to happen when, the way their worry is stylish. Olivia is not, in fact, ultra-concerned. Books have stopped mattering entirely. Before, they mattered. They were the diversions from horror, rooms made out of paper where you can hide inside of what has been written, alone. A book comes with a lock. Here is so public. The bathrooms! Reading is public. The classes.

I hate everyone, she thinks, but in the next moment she is knocking on Adele and Beth's door across the hall which has a mezuzah. A singular slanted chime nailed in. Better than the whiteboards hung up on everyone else's doors, where students draw erect penises going direct into markerbeards of brown grass. There is no whiteboard hung up here—a defiance. Against the University of Pennsylvania.

Olivia, bleeding, carefully checks her thin fingers for menstrual blood and then touches the mezuzah before knocking again, a custom she knows by now, seen frequently down the hall. All you have to do is look. Adele and Beth are both home and tell Olivia that they do not have *The Rainbow*, neither of them studying English this semester.

"We are both pre-med!" says Beth, the younger sister, pipping from behind Adele. Beth is taller and beautifuler, not gruff like her sister, who is too terraqueous. She sometimes pips so high, leaping off the burlap of Adele's thick demeanor. Adele is the sterner sister, a sophomore who so gruffly mothers her one-year-younger sister, stoutbreasted and with pimpled double chin. Short of being bearded. Beth still has a chance. To shine.

"We need to go," Adele. "We're going to the mikveh. Do you want to come?"

"She has to read *The Rainbow* by tomorrow!" Beth squeals, also imitating the stylish concern for those getting things done in the hallways of the dorms of the University of Pennsylvania, but imitating in a failing way, not hitting *at all* on the exactness of the beast of what it is, which is the University of Pennsylvania, the specific tone of money tingling, the malaise of having things.

"Are you done with your menstruating?" Adele needs to know. Because every naked part of them will have to be touched by the holy water, every hair and pimple, chin. That is the rule.

"What is a mick . . .?"

"We couldn't get synchronized in our bleeding again forever, and then Adele had to go over to the pool alone and then I had to walk alone, too."

It has been awful for Beth! New to Philadelphia from the suburbanness north, full of pippery, bright stars down her spine, but frightened by walking alone. But here in West Philadelphia there is green foam between each maroontooth of brick, and for this, she did like to walk even alone, heathenous as it feels under a heavenous so silverous! Pip! But she wanted to bleed when her sister did again as they had, all summer going to the mikveh without their mother, but their flows had separated, a river's fork between them when joining this particular dorm floor after August's preparatory semester.

"We have always been on the same menstrual schedule but something has happened," Beth pips again from behind Adele, whose tuba-boned seniority adds: "Which we had to do. Because of Sabbath and the elevators. What about yours? Are yours regular down here?"

It has been a dorm hall topic. Every girl has had her period interrupted, overblown and smashed in, and divided, drips and globs of blood over the weekend, then nothing, and then a gush, as if the moon lived a dorm room down from them, turning itself over, controlling everyone. Ripping the blood rivers into scatters. There is talk on the whiteboards about it. And gossip in the stalls. Olivia closes her eyes as she walks toward the toilet. Her menstruation is an utter defecation of blood if she waits too long to empty herself of tampons. She weeps often over the toilet. There is no one she can call. She doesn't want to hear her mother.

"A mikveh is orthodox," Adele tells her gruffly. She has her mandatory University of Pennsylvania black peacoat pulled tight over an already-flopped-over bosom, and then a long skirt underneath, wool, her shoes the color of dour, upturned tools. She is Amish, Olivia decides. There is no difference.

"After orthodox women menstruate, we visit a pool. If you are done bleeding, you can come."

It has rained and the streets of West Philadelphia have become very charming, the bricks swaddled in sopping orange organza. Olivia does not want to menstruate into a pool. But Beth flutes—

"Come with us! It doesn't take long!"

On the walk, Adele is quick, stout, her head down like the Amish women working in the factory's long kitchen, hair covered, saying their prayers, indignant and insistent—dull. Beth will be Olivia's friend. They walk behind, admiring the doused trees, the leaves delivering rain on their arms and necks as a way of at last reaching out to these two freshmen, finally touching their necks and arms. What these trees have wanted.

Olivia, bleeding, who is not done bleeding at all, made sure to excuse herself to the dorm's bathroom first, to survive the walk at least, pushing in three more tampons and then, without thought, braiding their strings as if preparing a girl for school. She pulled up her underwear and flushed without looking, the burbling violet pond so quickly created there in the bowl, the used tampons bobbing like the bloated limbs of the dead in *War and Peace*, the war parts, which most students in her class confessed to having skipped over, only reading the sections on marriage, or Peace, but Olivia had appreciated seeing men bleed.

"Do you have a boyfriend?" asks Beth.

"No," says Olivia. The teaching assistant keeps asking a similar question, the buttons on his blazer trembling, too young. She feels her teacher too young.

"Do you want to eventually go to medical school?" she asks Beth, who also seems very young. She feels the ancients in her own blood, spilling out.

"Yes," Beth says in the style of joyful confession, the outbreak of your soul in public. But she is not sure. She is not very queasy around blood, but they made her look at a cadaver on the tour! They made her look at it carefully and touch certain parts with gloves. The bloodless man. Emptied. She had never seen a penis before. She was vomiting in the toilet and they asked her, "Do you want to switch majors? Do you want to be an English major?" They were proud. They'd looked and touched. They were full of their contented malaise, looking over the flesh, stylish. Their eyes were annoyed, and glad. Gold lidded. "What do you want to do?" they asked her. In a fake hurry with her that was leisure, *utter.*

"I want to go back in," Beth assured them, and she looked again and touched the corpse and was fine. It wasn't his body. It wasn't even his grayness! It was fine! It wasn't that he was incredibly fat. She had after all seen her sister parading around their dorm room naked! The skin hobbling down that bottom. It wasn't that his heart no longer was working, or that his mind was now missing. It wasn't that people are supposed to be buried and not left to sit out on tables. It was his thin cock! Its thinness in comparison to his fatness. You lift a tuba, and voila! A little pin. It made her puke.

She could get over his cock like a talis, no talit, female, she willed. She pipped! But now, she tells Olivia, she actually *likes* to watch the operations. "There is one physician here," she says, "Dr. Edelberg, who lectures every evening. He says he enjoys students, even freshmen, being in the amphitheater," she beams. Shines. She's had sex dreams. She dreams the doctor in her. His cock has been a velvet surgery. She's been smoking a mezuzah in the bed afterward, the sheets full of ram's blood. He's offered her a light. He's lit her little torah. He's cut out her heart with his cock. This is sex. Her vagina doesn't exist.

She imagines telling Olivia all of this. She imagines a friend.

"Look," Adele tuba-barks back toward them from her pressing-on hunching. "Read that for class, Olivia!" And it is true, a rainbow, over the West Philadelphia trees, dripping, piped over the University of Pennsylvania, over malaise, something strange in the evening hour. In early fall. A miracle.

"I will!" Olivia shouts.

"It's ok," Adele tells her at the pool. "Everyone gets naked and it's fine."

Adele, as if to show this is terribly true, reveals her own bush so brown and dry-blood crusted, the lips underneath the fur so hanging, the clitoris limping out of the hair like a rooster's drip of throat, so Olivia begins to feel better, confident. She looks at Adele's baggy vagina, abstract of her pimpled, doubled chin, irreconcilably bearded below her, and feels fine, *almost more orthodox.*

They briefly visit the bathroom, where Olivia pulls her tampons' braid down over the toilet, releasing the three blood soaked stumps. She will hold it all in. She will *will it.* She is fine. She is full of malaise and ease. She pours her thin, naked form into the water. This is happening. She is no longer bleeding. It was Bethlehem that bled her, and she is seen now at night at the University of Pennsylvania, down the street, down Spruce, the University of Pennsylvania's closest mikveh, pouring herself into the pool. There is a young mother sleeping in the corner, her own bush a downturned cypress. Not much hair on the outer thigh. Another girl, younger than everyone, has hairy thighs. She closes herself, her eyes. She opens her eyes when Beth begins praying and notices there is no drain. It is like not seeing the moon. She tries to pray with Beth, humming along. She looks at Beth, who opens her eyes and looks at her. But then they close their eyes. More praying. Adele is grunting to pray. Olivia, bleeding, is humming. She tries. When they all open their eyes, the water is not water any longer. It is a rainbow writhing and thickening, its colors swirled and full-bodied. The three pupils of the University of Pennsylvania see everything. The rainbow is so bloodthick in the Jewish bath, so ironic you can walk on its back.

Adele,

It has been a harrowing year without you, you don't know. I went to the mikveh alone with Mom, who was in the pool and had gone dull. Your mother could not move! She could not feel—a dog, running its tooth down her myelin. What is myelin? It is nervous coating, it is butterfly butter, Adele. A dog ate her coat! And Adele, without you, I couldn't move her from the ladderless pool, and could not call. I was fearful to call, to spatter the tiles, the orthodoxy, with Multiple Sclerosis!

Adele, you could have lifted her out, with the strong arms you have, your grufflengths. Adele, you could have shoved her, the body, my mother, from the water, had you been here still and not premedical in your major at the University of Pennsylvania. (I am coming to you this summer!). But I could only float with her. I could, with my slimstrength, keep her only above a horizon of oxygen.

Adele, when new women came to plunge into the water, they saw her slumped in my hugging and they got men who wouldn't pull her, our body, your mother, pruned and purple leather, from my arms. Their eyes were squeezed, they were juicing their iris, so vigorous, so not to see us, and nobody would help, would touch a notwife, notmother, their coats felt, their dry hands. I hugged her, the longest hug ever, while she herself hollered for more women to come, and the women pulled her, four of them, fourbearers. I couldn't do it. She never told me I needed to—she only hugged for too long. The hug in its rags told me what this was.

Love,
Beth

Dr. Edelberg lectures on vivisection. The fall semester is always, he says, unhuman. They sit in the amphitheater together, freshman and sophomore, and stare down at him, who lights a candle. Nightlecturer. They call the amphitheater Dreaded Circle, the shape of watching, the blank table bloodcleaned, noonlamp above it, sole window, now moonlampen, seating for everyone, in the round. We must look like nothing, dark marks in the chairs, ink moanings. He lectures, his notes neatly out, four separated pages on the vivisection of a buck. The window has been shaken full of stars. Beth pips:

I believe him! I do not want to go to the bathroom. I do not want to be anything but a surgeon. Dinner, she remembers, in the cafeteria again, the kosher cemetery of foodplots to its left, the brutelumps, a knish. She wondered there where Olivia had been—Olivia, who never eats at Beth and Adele's hour. Beth misses her, already, so much, and looks up, where one does when one is full of insoluble sensation. Always.

Beth takes notes:

Animals are our future, particularly deer, not bear, amphibium of all kinds, not bison (gone!). We find out about the heart from them—the velvet on a buck's antlers—because if you tie a certain artery of the heart, I write, it can't send it the velvet any longer—so the antler becomes bare, but, the heart can turn, and velvet can return—I want that buck, not notes! Killed and splayed here, pastpanting. The antlers are severed and passed around, and the organs are given to the boys to suck on with their knives, to adore.

I want his bones. The moon is in the window now, the full damp mirrorskull.

Dr. Edelberg moves on to Womb Duplicatum.

"Dr. Edelberg, can Womb Duplicatum be cured? Can you remove this problematic womb, the second one, which you say lies behind the first, smaller and more furious, a mutation, from living women?"

"We are remaining in the domain of vivisection for fall. Ask again in spring, if premedicine is still in your thinking."

In Glen Park there was a statue of William Penn similar to the one affixed to the top of Philadelphia's city hall. Both representations held sheathed swords that, from certain angles of looking, appeared to be their erect penises. In Glen Park's park, sitting on a bench close to William Penn, who stood, was the Quaker hero George Fox, and he bent forward at the angle of momentous talk, toward Penn. They related to one another in their bronze way. But it looked like William Penn was going to stuff his erect penis into George Fox's baggy, eager mouth.

Children of Glen Park's park turned into adults while looking at this sculpted arrangement. At one point, you were a child. You were sitting on the bench beside George Fox, using his knee to hold your doll or chalking hearts on his cheeks. And then you saw it. You understood what the others had been saying. You understood an erection and what a blowjob is. You couldn't ever see it any other way. You never did again, in the park of Glen Park, the park you spent your youth in if you grew up here, seven miles northeast of Center City—up Broad Street and through fields, past the synagogues, the temples, then past Protestants, but not as far north or east as Mennonites, and nowhere near Amish. You, in the Quaker tuck of land, north of Unitarians, their deep slopes of ivied yards, south of mountains, north of flatness, east of Ohio—the aged oak trees south of pines, north of palms, west of algae—the grass soft on pouch-shaped land, the green grass short as fizzing, south of farming, north of paving, west of foam.

The central park of Glen Park is where you were handheld taken as a child. Beyond the park there was just more park, park wending into farmland, houses barely in rows, or on roads, an area that gave the impression of farming—a town of doctors getting their cut of country. There were pickets there that cornered no beasts. Each generous share of grass was empty of beasts and roots.

Minds were all there was in Glen Park, the soil salivating to be worked, but here were thoughts, everyone's father some kind of doctor, real surgeons, men who cut for a living, pruning tumors, milking uteruses, shearing lungs, clipping veins. There was the heart. They took their knives home in long briefcases with gold latches. They weren't for opening, but you knew knives rested there, the ones that had bccn dippcd in pcoplc, in strangc womcn. You wanted to shake the briefcase like a puzzle case, to determine its pieces, to think you'd solve them into a picture of your father, if you could open it up, if he would let you.

You were, at first, proud.

You understood your father's profession, head surgeon and professor of anatomy at the University of Pennsylvania, to be a great thing. But then you were also scared. You feared him committing surgery on you while you slept. You thought he'd tiptoe into your bedroom with his briefcase of knives, disassemble the latch, and start in. Notch your heart. Carve off your nose. You didn't know. You didn't know why he took the knives home. Why he clinged to his profession, or coyly threatened you, which is what you really suspected, but couldn't articulate, not even to yourself. Glen Park was a cowless earth. Farmed, if farmed, a century ago, by Penn, whose house had been given to him before you were born. Long swathes of grass and cowlessness.

And here was the park of Glen Park, where you went, though there were many fields, whole acres just for children's work: the playing fields. Worms often revealed themselves in these fields, and children ventured out to them as though wading into the sea. They wanted to wear them as red bracelets, or red necklaces—long, lugubrious jewelry. They slapped each other's faces with them, and flung them up into the air so they looked like wet, lost pieces of sunset.

But the people here were city people, come up here in a flight, people who fled the city and also their own Jewishness, like your father, now posing as farmers and Quakers, their houses barn-shaped, or silo-styled, their weekend clothes like those of workmen's. They flocked to the central park of Glen Park, because people want to gather in the round, around statues. They ignored a thousand fields that were square wending into rectangle wending west, opting just for this—a civilized circle.

Glen Park's park is where you, if you were Dr. Edelberg's daughter, were taken. It was in this park that you would lose your teeth, those square bonesamples, and name wild animals, and spin too rapidly even for you, and you would have thought that you were in the woods, but you were among *a single tree*, and you picked from the garden path, putting asphodels in your play purse, surprised to find them brown and chewed a day later. And here you showed your underwear, the soft undertuft of an angel wing, the ironed soulbell of a dove, gentle, true, and sometimes wet, sometimes full of yellowbells, juiced daffodils. And sometimes here you hid, going down into that circle of bushes, and it was here you spoke with an animal in a language parallel to language, and here you squirmed in the dirt, your tongue touching the dirt, tasting it as burnt chocolate, and here you looked at the sky, the blue prairie that was shiny—*not a cottonpatch for miles*—and you thought to remember death, from what you learned being born, from what you thought you kept hearing, and from the sun, that death is the end of life, that death takes life, and then you sprang from the bush not unlike a flame springing from a bush, a tart, loose lash, a yellow dress. You ran through your father's eyeballs. But his watching became intolerable. You leapt from him. The eye is just a thing of the brain, is a colored bubble blown off of the brain. And it is in aloneness that you realized William Penn was trying to stuff his dick inside George Fox's face. You saw everything.

Beth meets Antigone in the elevator, on a Saturday. She is going to the top floor of their dormbuilding for no reason. It will feel like flying! I'll take it up and down, basement to height, again and again. Hotfreight. She's burning. She burns with the fever of her reasoning, for not going. To Synagogue! Adele going to Synagogue, dourly dressed and vigorous. Beth in the slim bed—cough, cough. Adele's hand on her head, her pimplous palm.

"You're not feverous—you can come."

"Can't!" Pip. Rosh Hashanah in the fall semester, then Yom Kippur, one, two—"I'll come then, for those." She littlesisters.

Adele wonders what Olivia is, if not a Jew, if on their floor. Why here? What other reasons are there to be against elevators? "You'll feel better, Beth, being there." Adele gruffs, gruffmothers. Grandmothers. Shtetls. She makes a show of putting tissues in her purse, like their mother would if she went. Any longer. Adele stomps on any flower. She scrapes the dewy lugubrious licentious moss off of the bricks of West Philadelphia.

But Beth rolls over, plays ill, moms. I can't come!

But then, Adele gone, she takes the elevator in her pajamas, her leastdour outfit, colors, savoring pushing 7. She savors yellowlights. The electricity brazen and cozy around me! On the third floor, enter Antigone. They are the same alarming size, slimtwins, both nosed, the mangled fins off of ancient sharks on both of them, Beth's mangled to the left and Antigone's not. Right. Antigone pale, Beth dark, Sephardic, brownshining, Antigone's translucence, veins the baggy shadows of blue spiders.

"We're wearing similar pajamas!" Beth cries.

In Antigone's room she tells Beth of Quakerism:

"At a Quaker meeting there's no leader. You sit quietly together, and sometimes you stand and share."

"I'm supposed to be at synagogue right now," Beth confesses, Catholic in the face of new friendship.

"I feel ashamed of those men!" She tells her new friend, if Antigone will be my new friend, about the men who would not lift Mom, Adele, about how hard it was to hug and hold and tread the water, Adele, how hard it is to touch your naked mother. They left, Adele, the two men who even dared to enter. The others were still outside. If they had opened their eyes, they'd have to bury their eyes! For years. Oh, unhelpful orthodoxy! The women were helpful, finally, the new naked women, who hadn't plunged yet, my mother slumped in my arms, paralytic—I gave them her armpits and they gripped her up, one of them younger than me but stronger. A gruffteen.

They hold a Quaker meeting in the room. They do cocaine, brought up from 3. Antigonean Saturnine. They do it on a mirror that seems maintained for this, breakfastless. They sit on her floor.

But the cocaine makes them feel talkative, so they stand up and share. Saturdaydorm! "But no commenting," Antigone orders. "At a Quaker meeting, you can't enter into a conversation. It's just whatever you say and what the next person says." She puts more cocaine up her nose. She likes to bend down to catch it, to feel the aggression of her nose, jewbone nearing the mirror, becoming larger, more bent, more Jewish, bent rightish, an ancient kiss. "Remember, we're Quakers, so don't comment."

Beth sniffs only a small amount of cocaine. She, too, likes to bend over the mirror on the floor, the submission! It feels like standing up, this bending in, like something standing. She sniffs to rush the submission she is feeling, to push it in, like swallowing someone, cocaine, like groundbone. She snarls with feeling! She stands:

"I'm in love with my professor, Dr. Edelberg, a doctor. A surgeon!"

"But how do you know? How do you even say that?" Religion is for breaking. For shoving into a pyre of conversation.

"I'm in love, too. In Glen Park where I'm from. I went to visit him at night, past my father's sleeping, holding my breath by his door.

"William Penn lived in our house once, building it of log and then stone, improving on its frame, and a hair of his was even entombed under some varnish on the stairs. As a child, I would visit this curl of hair, the preserved lock, and touch it, my finger riding the curl, a fleeting path in the gloss. 'What are you doing sitting on the stair?' my father would announce. He could hear me sitting there.

"I went out at night alone all the time. To do this, I dismantled the chimes on the door, my father's device to keep me in, and I wouldn't have that! I took the chimes down from their wire loops. I put the stupid tubes in my pockets and went out. William Penn was waiting for me, and so perhaps was his friend, George Fox.

"Fox did not found Pennsylvania but was a premiere Quaker in England and he would visit Penn, in Glen Park, between being imprisoned, often. They would go out to this park and talk, Fox sitting down on the bench and Penn standing, just like this. A plaque says as much.

"I liked to stand right between them. No one was ever around. Midnight is not Quaker hour, nor kosher! You could do anything. The park looked like it was baking, puffing from its soil, stars darkened in the grass, disguised as stones. I picked up a star, and slaughtered asphodels.

"I spoke to Penn, sometimes totally ignoring Fox, and at other times including him. Playing a game with their emotions. They spoke to me in my mind as I looked at them so that I heard their voices disguised in such stillness.

"And what did they say?

"Oh, they gave me more information about Quakerism! But mostly, Penn was loquacious, and spoke about the founding of Pennsylvania, about the making of Glen Park's park, where he put what flowers and this bench, and digging ponds, and also more about living in his house. He had lived in my room. 'Your father hears you going, you know,' he told me, but I ignored that. He said, 'I used to sit in his room, my study, all night, up, so up!, and I used to think about maps, mapping my pond in its wood, now drained, and I would draw my maps and run my hands on them as a young person's responsive spine, and tear them up, for want of a walk.'

"George Fox was whispering to us.

"I wanted Fox to be quieter even. I wanted to only hear from Penn. 'But what was it like in my room? What happened there?'

"'I went there in the mornings after a night in my study and slept until it was late, so that I would look at my large clock and it would scare me, the alignment of its arms, and I would look outside and at the light, and I took my walk and then went into my study and wrote letters to constituents and governments, and to Fox. On Wednesdays and Sundays, there were meetings.'

"'But more about my bedroom!' I begged. I was touching his skin. He had bellskin, bell-made clothes. A sword.

"'You mean did I have Friends? Yes, I had Friends, though perhaps I would call them visitors. No, they *were* Friends, come from the meetings, on Wednesdays and on Sundays, visiting my room. I told them I liked what they wore, and removed what they wore, and experienced them in silence, Jesus continuous through us, though I know your father tries to forget Jesus's part in the light! Many were married. They all had other children. I was nothing but their moment in my room. I measured them, comparing my feelings upon them. How did it feel with one and then another? How did it feel to do one thing and then another thing to one thing? Pleasure did praise us often. And sometimes they were with my children, which is like looking at noon, at confrontation. But I was only a statue, gentle and unyielding, and hardfriended when needed. I could, like a grave, be visited.'

"'George Fox, what do you think?' I asked. And the sitting down statue began to answer me with his baggy stillbell lips, and my mind covered him over. I kissed and kissed Penn's mouth, using my tongue against bronze, forget Fox! I wept for their position. That he were sitting in his study again, my father found dead, and he coming then into my bedroom. His room. No one is talking. But I had to visit him in the indignity of the outdoors. I kissed him ferociously. Before coming to college, the night before I came here, I let him fuck me, his only gesture. He had no flesh, but I loved him. I kissed his freezing lips, trying to warm them, holding his face, feeding it my blood where it warmed within my fingers, until my fingers were freezing and the face was blushing. It seemed, under the moon, possible. It was possible, I thought, that he saw this, that his open eyes were opened by my thoughts. I allowed William Penn to enter me entirely, his cock, which he preferred to offer to George Fox, now into me, up touching me, my body clinging to him, his cock strong—'Oh, William!' I whimpered, practiced, and dreamed. I wanted to say, 'I love you.' I didn't want to leave him. Goodbye for now, I thought, and fucked him harder, with more passion, my insides churning warmth around the freezing length of metal at midnight. I stared into the curved, coinish eyes of my lover, in awe of the quivering happiness I could conjure, my pink flub of clitoris now tremulous, the drooping flub now flexible, a fire of feathers, internal, a pink blur, turned into a violet feeling of an air-wired almond in my anus, turned feather again, now pink smoke in my stomach, now the flub sobbing, now muscle-hearted glitter, my heart with the feeling of a tingling balloon, and then: alchemy of an orgasm, wood into golden, a stone flaming. Star risen. Penn's sword was dripping with blood, a red, boneless bird dissolving down his thigh, and I had to wipe it clean with my underwear in this park now public, morning's publication, this vandalism of my fucking. Love is vandalism."

Adele finds Olivia easily, on Tuesday. She knocks harder than Beth has—Beth's bright, faint knocks. She asks. For Olivia. Who answers after some time, after she packs the puffbag of diapers into her closet behind clothes and after she strips her sheets of robinmurder from the bed and puts new ones down, extralong, covering the growing pond behind them, the dryingbrown oblong below her pelvis which the sheets, the diaper, the pad, the underwear, and multiple tampons can't ever absorb. She puts her diary in a drawer, *War and Peace* on the shelf, and *The Rainbow* on the pillow, and holds her uterus, binarious, and speaks to herself. She says: "It's Adele."

She opens the door.

It is evening, before a lecture, Beth at kosherdinner, the cafeteria full of their jewfloor. The dormhall is quiet at seven, as the first floor girls care to eat, involving prayer, prayers, together.

"Do you want to sit in my computer chair?"

The computer chair, Olivia knows, is full of blood, but it is black and it has dried, and she has placed on it a coverlet, like one for bread. There are plenty here, the kosherfloor. And candles allowed on this floor, the extinguishers set to Off, the graciousness, the accommodations of the University of Pennsylvania to those who are orthodox, who use fire. "Prayer is for strong people," Adele offers. "My mother, who is sick, doesn't use it any longer. Religion is for the healthful. I do it now, is all, to distinguish myself from her being ill, from being too weak. Religion is for the able. That's all. A distinction. I pray for her, but only to say I'm not ill."

"Does Beth pray?" asks Olivia. "I mean, does she practice?" Some of the girls falling off, parents buried in a little distance—some girls enjoying elevators, cocaine, Olivia has seen. She saw Beth going, in an intermission from the bathroom, her bathroom Saturdays. Olivian, everyone gone praying, Olivia in the bathroom, her bathroom—God works if he gives me this. She switches toilets, luxuriating on her porcelain saturdayveranda, holy deckchairs, reading and flushing, tamponless for hours, blood as coagulate as an organ, jellied livers, diverse, redcompendium, greenbecoming—and violet in the last toilet. She saw Beth while planning a dash downhall, to gather *War and Peace*, which really was due soon—Natasha on her windowsill gaping at Heaven's frothy bottom—if I could have such a sill! Porcelain, with a hole, from which to gape at Heaven, alone from . . . and Beth was small in her pajamas before the buttons, up or down (a basement with washing machines), and Olivia shrinking back into her bathroom, the one time it is mine, stars musterable on the rustmottled ceiling. The eyes are not nothing! Are the coachmen of every heavens.

"Beth prays but she uses all of it wrong, to sing," Adele offers. "And she uses the mikveh to swim. To take a walk in the evening. She uses everything abusively. Her lecture notes are . . . lacking in information."

"She has been looking for me." Olivia is turning pale, turns pale at night, and bright. She needs the bathroom. She excuses herself, the hall still gentle with emptiness. In the stall she removes four tampons, all full, hemoglobin and serum, and they unfurl in the bowl, sheep, their stomachs bit, blood and blue in their wool. She flushes her fourflock, the helpful animals she kills—and panics. New tampons forgotten! Adele in my dorm room.

"Excuse me. I have to go back there for a moment."

"To the bathroom?"

Adele is reading *The Rainbow* on the bed. Shoes off. "This is so flowery."

"Oh, purple." The teaching assistant called it that. "I can't read it. I can't concentrate."

"I thought it was due—that you had to already." Olivia remembers Adele's body, its pride and thrust and lumps, its pimpled pouches and fingers thick as though bandaged. Her hairiness, the rough, outrageous bush, and the clitoris that dripped crookedly out from the coiled leavery, a rodent's little liver, what she imagined of the bedraggled lung of something waterous, a barracuda's ripped reason for breathing, hanging into the open, with rancid coral hueing—again, Olivia begins feeling fine. Better. I bleed effusively, I do, but from something simpler, I'm sure. She hadn't looked. But imagined it was fine, finned—a nothing, pink hem. And she had not grown much hair. She had not grown much of anything at all. She crawls next to Adele's pimples and chins, breasts Amishish, uninteresting, and Olivia orders, imperial and glad, better and bold, "Read aloud." And Adele does—she reads the flowers. She tries to spit them, purplesputum, but the flowers keep billowing and piling. "It's not a problem," Adele says about the bleeding. The bed. She says it again, is effusive somehow, a note growing in the gruff. "It's not a problem to me at all."

"Why isn't it a problem?" Olivia moans, comfortable. "There's blood everywhere. It's getting all over. I can't stop it."

Olivia had been at the factory on a Sunday when her two wombs commenced their initial menstruation. Her father's youngest horses were developing softness in their hooves. They needed to be shod in diapers, an Amish method. But he could not get any Amish. They were at their church or at home, and his wife and his daughter were not practitioners of anything, nothings—and her mother was frail. "Ask Olivia," his wife, sick, suggested. She called from her bed, "Olivia!"—who hated to be called. To be called is to be unheard. Olivia was hiding, reading.

She was hidereading poetry!

They drove in the Benz with a magnitude of diapers, acrylic clouds tidily folded. She was fourteen, too old to start bleeding. But she hadn't earlier. Too thin.

"I hate to be called at," she confessed to her father, and he was nothing, silent, opening his low and heavy gate, the factory always visible above it from anywhere you looked. You could see it.

His youngest horses were rotting with an infection from poor conditions. You could see it. The hay scattered in a gesture. These were not stalls or an industrial ode to barns but a circular room in the center of a dome, innard of a black tongue-ripped bell—steel—where the stinking skin of young horses milled on bone, beleaguered, the larger ones in a divided area you couldn't call stalls.

You work alongside your father—your use revealed at last, revealing yourself. You show you are, in your bold heart, a grown man, as shrewd and capable as him, forgiven, at last, for who you were. You were his daughter.

"You have to get behind them and grab their hooves," he explained to the person. He handed Olivia her first package of diapers.

Olivia lifted their legs, the young tremble lengths, gaunt and shy. They responded to her light touch. They trusted the weakness they felt in her fingers, like thoughts or grass, not force. Invisible flowers. She hoped he would watch. Watch this success! She taped the diapers on each hoof.

"Be rougher," he told her from across his enclosure, the innard-ripped blackness. Rougher is quicker.

"And then what will we do?" she asked. She wanted to show an interest. As he had not shown, not asked what she was reading in the Benz. She had wanted this interest. His. She would show him how to love.

"Then everything else we have to do today." He used a short knife.

The way he talked to her, she could be anyone. Anyone, not a daughter. A worker. Whatever. She should have kept reading! To read is to look down. Is to refuse. She wanted her book! It was in his Benz. She wanted to shortknife his heart. She'd knife it with a book.

Olivia felt a boiling violet kick in her underwear.

She hurried down to the big empty kitchen, her inside thighs covered in a brunt of blood, and there she tried to wad a napkin under the source, and then a mixing bowl from the kitchen, filling the bowl three times more and pouring it down the toilet, then each toilet in the long bathroom's line with a bowl in each hand. Two bowls. She said that the toilets were cows who need blood, and she was here for them, helping these cows, pouring help into the white narrows below toilet bowls, inversion of their udders. Mothers! She was only eighty pounds.

Olivia ran back through the factory, clanging down the bell to find diapers, she remembered! She needed one. If they were all used already, on the horses, she'd have to rip one off a hoof— and she planned this—but only found them floating in a room full of blood, and like a girl finding a room full of girls, you know this room is yours, and where the blood like her blood set like a sunset through the float of acrylic nebulous and into the drains to terraqueus, she stood above and profusely contributed. She tore down her underwear and threw it nowhere like red swan skin into the mire of bloodletting, the bunches of flesh, the wads and strips of blackened skin, and all the other guts luscious and bobbing, glazed, in the sopping lowering. This is what it looked like, Olivia thought, to stand on top of where the sun drains down. Light, when it moves, is the blood of young beasts being used. You see everything—except for any bone. That has all been taken away.

Adele puts down the book. She has been holding it above the bed, to keep it from blood. Olivia is small like her sister, genetic tremblelength in a stout pool, little mistaken willow. The pink etch of her forearms.

Adele gruffs, "So where were these bones taken? What kind of factory was this?"

"I don't know!" Olivia lies.

"You know," Adele gruffs, kisses, "you're Olivia—O beautifully bleeding—Knox."

The horses up at Bethlehem Knox had not been buried. The horses were unzipped and de-boned, their legs chopped off and then the hooves, on later tables, removed from those. But there was no time for burial, the way business was moving. There was land. Harold

Knox. Did not want all of that land, or not for the simple use of its stomach, for digestion of boneless beings. If he was going to buy land, he wanted to build and not bury, and he did this, buying up Bethlehem, and building it a factory, the black steel onion, almost balloon curved, but hissing smoke, horsesmoke.

The bones were dealt with separately, and men prided themselves if they could work with the bones, not the flesh, the better material, the white pulled prize amidst the spoiling grubflesh of inedible—or unsellable—meat. Carcasses in the deflated shape of horses—no, the bonemen did not envy their meatbrothers. The bonemen scoured the dirt and blood off the ribs, skulls, joints, spines, and hooves—the hooves being best. The ground bones were filler around the hoof importance, the hot keratin that makes food puff with ballooncells, that makes meat float.

The men ate gelatin creations for lunch: molded avocado and tuna, waldorf salad elated in a vinegar suspension, jellied veal loaf, the veal rump lifted through pureed celery stalk in blissful, blissing particles, creamed chicken with the sparkling black of pepperstarriness. For dessert there were cups of tingling mousse, chiffons, snows, whips and creams, charlottes and no-bake soufflés.

They said that keratin is *not* the ingredient. Harold did. Bethlehem Knox officially said. He said, "There's only keratin in a horse's hoof, and I need only the tightly coiled protein of bones, pigs and cows mostly." But the horses were shipped, were scalped from the hills.

Bethlehem boomed, and so did Pennsylvania, more men coming in, more families being born, peopling the churches and schools, children growing, knowing their profession as one knows of coming home. Very few people died. The factory was safe. Harold left his prominent mansion to visit it often, visiting the men, making sure. They were safe. And the women—were Amish, from farms just southwest, those whose pies and kitsch didn't sell well at Reading Terminal, the market in Philadelphia, needing something else. He offered this.

The steel onion was subdivided inside, each room with a processing purpose, a need for deboners and burners, cleaners, and grinding men, men who worked the blades with their hands, and mixing men, mixing the so-potent keratin with less-so protein, bucketeers, men who packed powder into giant white buckets, and then these things were shipped—at first, everywhere.

There were no killers. The horses couldn't be killed. You cannot kill a horse without disrupting its bone, and they used every bone. You can't shoot a horse. The horses were dead by default, death a byproduct of use, by knives, not guns. The men who deboned them did not kill them but deboned them, began a slit from the heart through the stomach, knives pained into the spoonbloats of their stouts, guts stiff and unyielding, at first, then tumbling onto washable floors. There was washing to do. Hosemen, coming in the morning, hosing blood into drains, hosing it into pipes that let blood into the ground, reddening the innards of the land for long stretches, causing townflowers to smell confusing, an unnamable conflux of minerals, and worms so large and red the children called them hellsnakes and wrapped them twice around their necks. But a carcass does not wash down a drain, the horsesuits lay crumpled, like coats removed from elaborate hangers. They were rotting costumes. The burning happened each day. Everyone saw the smoke. And had its gray flavor in their clothes.

The women. In the large, industrial kitchen, for more than one thousand men every day, they scooped powder straight from the buckets, into dishes variant and wholesome, going from the now-famous recipes in the gel-cookery books penned in name by Mrs. Knox. They were really written by scientists, foreigners, but Mrs. Knox had signed herself and signs them still, eternal. Though everyone knows she's ill. The men were served. Creamed, buoyant lobsters. On Christmas night, they ate a weightless turkey with silver spoons. The big kitchen was full of pregnancy, aprons nooning, women working into their ninth months, drinking Knox-mixed drinks for the good of their bones, and to regain their figures before birthing, to be more like Mrs. Knox, who, when pregnant with Olivia, Harold Knox reminded them, did not change at all, was small, wore her pregnancy like a purse you would strap around your waist for convenience. Someone should invent such things, he thought. Scornfully.

He blamed the one foul pregnancy on Mrs. Knox. At home, she no longer received any pleasure. She had become entirely sick! She lay in her bed under gold covers that could not conceal his poverty. The Amish woman felt to him unattached, her farm far southwest. Her husband was working, farming. Or was down at Reading. He fucked her, the Amishwoman, within the milling of lank, waiting horses, upturning her woolen clothing. Un-douring what at first felt wooden, but wood bloating into fruit. He tried ripping her bonnet.

When he was found on the floor of the factory, murdered, it was discovered he had not left any ounce, not a penny or its half, to Olivia. Or to Mrs. Knox. Because he had a son, and midnight hardening, a rainbowbrained rock, black, which August Haas held in his eyes, on a bus.

Adele is kissing her. Not her neck. They do it on the dormcarpet, facing west, south. Olivia thinks hopelessly, without control, of her mother. Her deadfather. How he was found. It's part of her passion, the pieces of him. And Adele's prayer—she thinks of that too—the distinction, a vigorous push off of a drowningwoman, Adele thinking—No, Beth, I wouldn't have helped you then, I would not have lifted her at all, I would have been like the men—and Olivia now fucks herself off of Bethlehem—reading doesn't work. Fuck books. She fucks. She fucks with her fingers and knees, kneading Adele's breasts, the failed challic droops, with her thighs. She lets herself be entered by Adele's gruff fingers with their melodious minor seizures, the joints shimmering in her, the fist a puff, softer than the finger, a tormentous pleasurepresence, a fibrous flexible cloud braised with blood. It flows from the elbows. Blood is on the floor, is through the door a little, is in Adele's mouth, is poppyoil, is rubydung, is robinbattle. Isn't wrong. At all.

"Do you know August Haas?" she asks.

"Nothing, no one," Adele murmurs, Beth gone. Let her be the surgeon, do cocaine. I will have Olivia. I will braid this girl. I will become nothing, or a doula. Olivia, your eyes are bleeding, just a little, not tears, around their rims, redlighting, something coming. She opens her fist on Olivia's stomach, as if something were compressed—a gem, a reason. There is none.

"Because he's here, at the University of Pennsylvania," Olivia insists, her orgasm duplicatum. "My father had a son."

Animals shitfucking behind the barn and near the kitchen. They were behind each other. There were at least a hundred of those cats, white or orange with pink perforations under their tails. Blubber around a hole. Su-Yon, at first, was like that to Luther Haas. He roughly picked her up to be examined as he did to cats on his family's farm.

He met her at the Reading Terminal Market in Philadelphia, on Tuesdays through Saturdays, where he went to sell the butter, jam, ham, and dolls with his father. August, his brother four years younger, was at home, doing nothing in the barn. Luther was the one who went to the city. And of being Amish—life is vertical, you see the sky and know why you work, and the sky milking your work, and milk living lit in the schtanna.

At Reading Terminal, a global market of goods in Philadelphia, across from the oversized and failed convention center, the Amish resided at one end, selling bread and kitsch, pies and kitsch, of their living life, and the rest of the world jumbled into the other, Italians on top of Thai. Su-Yon, a Thai teen, didn't want to leave her aunt's stand and go anywhere, to the car. Too private. You knew nothing about her. Thai Imperial Pagoda. PAGODA in red lights signifying cheap Chinese. But it was not cheap Chinese. Much better. Only one dish available. Salmon slab the size of a dorsal fin, over rice, with special sauce. $3.50.

God it was cheap. How could this salmon, salmon expensive and running out, the pink pieces of river ever reducing, come to such a price? How did Thai Imperial Pagoda make money? How did she even break even? How did Su-Yon, young and thin, with a garden green lash of color in her hair the milk of midnight, survive?

Some decided cloning, the business predicated on a single salmon. They have this salmon. This Thai lady—and her Thai teen, Su-Yon—have immigrated some special needles hidden in noodles, some scientific recipes or clauses. They have rebuilt the flesh of fish in the kitchen. They fry a hundred pounds of the same salmon each day.

Su-Yon's customers constantly asked her where the salmon came from. But she didn't understand enough English. She was fifteen. Five years older than my brother Awg, Luther noted, calibrating others against his August. And a year older than myself. He watched her shout out change and then hand back the change. She shouted the price and held out her hand, a yellow flower, a slightly moist daffodil, the fingers tight together to prevent loss. Su-Yon's customers and Luther's customers couldn't be more dissimilar. Those craving secret salmon with special sauce do not then crave unsalted butter in the big Haas-stamped buckets. Hauled by farmshoulder over the counter. Those wanting hot fish would not also like a white doll.

Luther met Su-Yon at last on the spitspattered pavement outside the Market, loading buckets into the truck going back. She smoked a violet cigarette which he had not seen before, and he asked her for a smoke-sip and gestured toward her fingers, which, at the end of her workday, parted and drifted, becoming loose and jaunty, liquid, mellow. Asking is so formal, he thought. I should just take it from those loose fingers, can stone down daffodils.

A Tuesday later she handed him a whole unlit cigarette, violet, over the jam rows and butter buckets. His father was turned toward University of Pennsylvania students who had come here on obvious assignments. The students took notes on the length of the beards here and the German brunt in his father's vowel, were anthropologizing without apologizing, their purses expensive. And Luther was eating his first piece of salmon, scooping it with a plastic spoon behind Su-Yon's stand, out of view. The fish was tender, excreted pink oil, peeled off in plump flakes. She tasted some jam and ate a swathe of butter he carried over to her on a little lid. She sucked a plaintasting stick of honey. He ate more salmon, a dozen of her salmon, asking for more salmon and cigarettes. She gave him salmon; she had plenty. She rolled him five, fifteen cigarettes. They smoked in the car. Then he jammed into her, forcing pinkblubber. She was a narrow area. It could barely smoke itself a violet, let alone have him in her, be shitfucked behind the barn or near the kitchen. In the car.

"She's tight," Luther told August in his barn where he hid. "She has these bruises on her back, but she says it's because of how she sleeps on the floor by her aunt. She's tight and so cold, her body is a bouquet of daffodils and daisies and yellowbells and two brownbells, and one mauve some kind of blooma that's been put in the cooler, like frozen fuck-opening flowers! I eat them.

"And salmon!" he said, tongue loquacious as a wing. "Salmon is great. I don't know what we're doing with butter, with pigs. Salmon is light and fruity, but with spices, like a spiced grapefruit, if grapefruit were—a bit more substantial."

Awg had never eaten fish, grapefruits, spices.

Su-Yon encouraged Luther in the backseat of her Aunt's truck with the burnt leather smell, like a chafed buggy, oleaginous moss growing on the footcarpet. He fucked her turned around, as he knew was done, had done, was clutching the ripped up seat stuffing, acrylic nebulous, stuffing her anus. "How do you make the salmon!" he teased, pulling her hair, her green lash, like a reign, creating a mock episode of customer frustration. "How are there so many fucksalmon! What did you do?" he screamed. "Tell me Su-Yawn, what's the story there?" Scared and cornered, she defecated when he left her. It followed him. She cried. "Change," she begged. She looked out the carwindow in the covered garage as though looking up at constellations. Her shit was writhing, two pieces. Pink pisces.

What he missed most were her cigarettes!

He thought of taking them from her loosened fingers outside of the market, or of taking Haas Family Butter money and buying them, but they weren't for sale. She wouldn't even sell him salmon any longer. She looked down. He searched through the barn floor one early morning before he had to leave, kicking the thin thatch of hay in search of leftover violetpapered butts, which he imagined chewing violently. He thought of the color violet and chewed. He kept on searching, searching even the stars though the sun was starting, was hissing a horizon, for her sinarettes.

"Su-Yon, why are you mad?" She didn't speak enough English. "What's so shitfucked?"

They were outside the market. His father was inside, closing their buggy-shaped stand down by himself. Used to it. Having a teenage son. Relax and he'll turn. He'll circularize to me. But to be seen by him now is to be diminished, scalped. My son the surgeon, removing even the organs—he'd sell them, my heart, for drugs.

As Haas closed their stand, closing the lids on buckets of butter, cleansing scoops, he consented to the violence. Luther is where? The violence of being left. At least tell me what you do! Luther led Su-Yon by daffodil, by hand, browning it with pressure, a little, to her aunt's car, the aunt also stripped and scalped and bagged up until this was done, Thai Imperial Pagoda gagged, the salmon and money killed and swathed. Only one thing is alive!

Su-Yon, alone.

He faced her in the car. Un-stripped creature. Sole interest. He stripped her. She turned but he turned her, gripping the shoulders and stilling any last tries to orbit out of this. "Do not turn around." The front was different. It was the difference between a pig hallway and lugubriousness, her hot fishlength. She said, "Please, Please!" but he couldn't please, and she didn't mean please. She meant other English. She stared as if she was schtanna, dutchstarlight, opening and closing her eyes. Blinks like passing clouds.

They lay together in the car, smoking at last her violet, and he asked, "What's in this?" tapping on the colored paper. It was something white inside that blackened and crawled into their mouths. She refused English, its practical tablets being offered to her by all of these Pennsylvanians who think they are doctors. They wanted to knife language in her. Barge it. She loved her cigarette. He tried to strip her face off with his eyes to see if she would disappear too. He tried to scalp her. Her skin shone. Starspattered. Daffodil silk, her cheek. Her black hair had the greenstained, sex shattered stem.

They are preparing for another evening lecture in the amphitheater, Dreaded Circle. Required. An important lecture on the blood, required. They are supposed to go home tomorrow, for the new year, October. Beth has not gone to Synagogue, is a cocainequaker every Saturday now, where there is no leader. Antigone and Beth taking turns kneeling over the small mirror, Beth's lines becoming longer, stouter, and Antigone still undecided in her major.

"All I know is I don't want to become any kind of doctor."

"Like your father."

They converse, breaking the meeting. Once kissed. Beth pipped that she wanted to brush, to brush Antigone off her mouth! She did, down the hall, she used Antigone's toothbrush.

The lecture this evening is to be on the blood—hemoglobin and serum, so much connected with life, students are to understand, that it is alive in its fluid state. Dr. Edelberg, promising us a basin to put our hands in. To watch our cuticles through!

"Are you going to dress correctly when we go tomorrow?" Adele, bundled in her pea coat, her hat, headbent. Beth in a scarf, a rapid Indian scarf! Streetbought . . .

"I'll dress as you do." She never sees Antigone otherwise. Otherwise, we are not friends. Haven't seen Olivia since the mikveh, to which I no longer attend. I swim in the gym! I walk alone most evenings, to the hospital where the lectures are given. Adele reads my notes, doesn't go, is busy, she says, with other studies. What? The Sprucepath to the hospital, the brickblanket, moon unfragile, hardfriend when in need, indeed—and moss more profuse in the corners of these bricks.

But she adds, "I'll dress as you do, fine, but Mom is not even going." To Synagogue. The sick don't celebrate. They are breathing.

"But we are." Adele. We're well.

The students circle into the Dreaded Circle, and wait for Dr. Edelberg's first candle.

A surprise in the fall semester, a cadaver! A woman old and thin, and black, deadexposed on the operating table, candlecornered. The flame carries this corpse in a brightbubble up to Beth's shining eyeball.

"Can you see?" Dr. Edelberg says, passing the flame down the form, bloodgone.

He begins his lecture: "The dead are useful. It is a challenge, I know, to disbelieve in humanpain, even in a deadperson." He takes his knife to her head. "To pass through skin," he lectures, "is passing through a barrier, like sound, and your knife must feel in these moments as regular to you and as invisible as your finger. As a thought." He does it. Passes through her, middling her. Nothing leaves her. Prepared. Dead. "Beth, come down here."

Beth trembles to be singled, to be called. I am only a freshman! She thinks of Antigone sneaking out past her professor and fucking William Penn! She sneaks toward Dr. Edelberg. The cadaver is fine, a woman. It was the man she could not handle on the pre-semester tour, that made her vomit! Penis, uncouth, too young on his person. Here, there is proportion, the breasts only a little asymmetrical, the vagina shaved—everything shaved—to reveal nothing terrifying, a hang of brown with pink between, something elfin. She likes this woman, black person. Mauve in her death, a souring blue underneath. Muddy cherries somewhere percolating in the deadloin.

"You are literalists, all of you, graphing this plot, the steps I'll take to extirpate an eye, a tumor of this breast, in my cutting off a cyst. You don't see past these steps, your books, but you must. You are all step. You want to watch and graph, graphing the position of my knifing. But you should be looking right at my mind. My decisionmaking, not my action. As I cut and move, you need to watch how I feel, how quickly I feel things, and decide. My actions are nothing—they are the moves—you need my mind."

Edelberg to Beth, "Alright, look into my eyes. They are two carriages. You can ride them through my brainflame. You will be sealed inside of them, away from any burning.

"In my eyes you are protected."

Beth pips into them! These eyes are dung tongues, bell-ends, brown unringing, rainbowrimmed. "Don't look at what is happening to this body, look at me, and don't become nauseated." Beth watches him and assists. To work alongside him, holding tenaculum or the muted skull down, or holding rag, dutiful, to a latesprung artery, while Edelberg's mind fills his fingers, it sends dogged darkbirds through them, and these fingerthings now mounting that knife, which is a horse galloping across humanbone on all this roadless rowing, the heart in the middle, the ruby circle still. Birth of July, Beth remembers. Unbeating. To work alongside your professor, Dr. Edelberg, is to love him! She is everywhere inside of him. A flooding bell in you I am, pipringing! And dutiful! "Here you are," he says to her, in front of everyone. Everyone watching. He speaks in Latin. "Touch." Touchus. The revealed heart is in her hand, wormvelvet.

The sisters need to pack, to get on the train. The train will be full, with all of them, woolenyoungwomen! Unlooking. She won't go, wants more Quakermeetings, more cocaine, which isn't kosher. Cocaine feels un-kosher. Her bones feel nauseous with churning fluorescence. She told Antigone, "You never were in love with anyone! William Penn? You've been in love with yourself, loving yourself before you left."

"No," her Saturdayfriend stared. "I was indeed fucking William Penn, and George Fox was watching. I loved to feel his eyes on me, to know he saw what I did to his friend while he couldn't move, or live. I know they are dead. I knew. But I fuck the dead, desirous still."

Her father had followed her, Antigone knew, in the rainbow-ink dark, and the moon moving squids in the clouds. He'd seen what she did. He was watching her, seventeen, the night before her leaving, fucking the statue of Penn. Voraciously. Her underwear a scalped dove floating in the leaves of that bush over there. Grass is the humblest flower. Almost dour. Bloomresistance.

Forcing him. Does she know he's not alive? What does she know? He was thinking. I will let you lead me, he had thought. But this is where? He wanted to call out to her. But what would he call out? "Stop! Ho!" She did not like listening. This daughter made the motion sometimes to rip off her ears! What was she thinking? Doesn't she know it is metal, nothing? Not a lover, not Person. Doesn't this hurt and disgrace her insides, of which she knows nothing? Penn is dead.

"He called to me, but I didn't listen. I couldn't hear, didn't care. I didn't care what he saw."

And now, Penn missing. "He was missing in the morning."

Penn was gone.

Gone.

Fox sat there. Antigone leaned, meager, meagered, kneeling, knees botched with grass, and Penn stolen! Where drowned? Missing. . .

"I felt the air, all over, with my fingers.

"And, Beth, he would not have left on his own volition!

"So where is he? I looked around, my father waiting in the morning, this dormroom waiting. Driving down. I admit it, his mind was mine, but where are you gone? Did my father remove him when he saw what I do? How is it his business? He should have been asleep. What else was I supposed to do with my time, with whom? Who else? I have no information. Where else? Penn lost?

"Beth, will you find him, where my father has taken him? Will you ask him?" Antigone, who has not been to any of her classes for weeks, who kneels by her mirror, to whiteworms unvelvetish, who sniffs, and sobs, and who has been too weak to kiss, her lips enormous with aimlessness, muscleless maw of wan-ness, a lame pollutant in her paleness, the tongue hidden or unwilling—Beth had found more lust in the gristled pricking push in her toothbrush!— now seeming to be just losing it.

"No," Beth tells Adele. "I've decided, I can't go. Dr. Edelberg has asked me, this Saturday, to prepare a skeleton for him."

She tells Antigone the same, a note on her board, on the bottom: "No, I can't come." Parenthesis. "I'll find Penn."

She creeps into the cadaver's room in the hospital's basement.

Breasts removed and head bald. The heart taken.

Could I shave the skin right off? No, that's not how I do it— think of Edelberg: you boil, at some point after cutting, you, boiling.

A cadaver's namelessness, elderly mistress, a public matter—she, released to us. I have already studied the uneven heart in my hand, and every animal this semester, and oiling my palm across livers, dull yellows, dogstomachs. And now I am here wanting a skeleton, beyond tedium, skin the tedium. Everyone if you use them, study them, and cure them long enough, is a bone. Hard outline inlaid in her—I want one!

Beth sets it into the water almost aboil. The eyes were removed, cut at the stem the flowerbubbles they are, sockets now filling. I want my first skull. The full clavicle. This is not some lecture with Dr. Edelberg standing over something else, a dog, a tree mouse, a butterfly cut across its lips. That buck once! This is not one of those early evenings, his flame basting his cadavers in bright butterponds. The moon is a bone.

Get to this one. Boil her and retrieve the skeleton as it bobs loose from her skin. Inconsequential coating—get it off. I never wanted to touch it. I never wanted to grip anything less than hard, compact shanks of white, batons, wanting to hold not breasts but lengths—to hold not her flesh but her joints—something that tells my hand, "I, too, am stern." I'm stern! Beth pips. She strips her, using hot water. Other students, the others here at the University of

Pennsylvania, even Adele, they don't need this. Adele does not. Let her rot. They don't need night—flesh is fine for them, as are organs and morning. They sit with their organs in their corner. But give me here, the bones, her bones to me.

She boils it, the skin clumping in lumps of brown and plum. The skull shows, a beginning, and the scalp, intractable resin, writhes away, and then her full skull, showing itself as a white-bottomed boat rolls over in dark water, its susceptibility to white boats. To boatwrecks. Such plum foam she makes! Such wool.

The skull now, and now her shoulders, the undressing. Beth retrieves the skimmer clearing the water, and more of it is shining, the shanks of stars, more white tilting upward into exposure, more alive than the boiling of water—shivering marionette in its hotness. And Dr. Edelberg will be down to check, to find this all done. These are for you. Beth lifts up the frame, small woman. He showed her, earlier, its tongue. "Look here," he said, and showed the tongue, a fainted flat branch. He had cut out her tongue! To further feed my palm.

Beth washes away the last of the skin, its easy comeupping now. The room smells of nothing, bone odorless, and just shining, bone Christmas. Her, Quaking. Quiet night. She puts a sheet over it and runs fingers not palms across clothsoftened clavicle, this bone veranda for a moment, bleached and ideal, for a moment like landing on a flat stretch of the moon, an impossibility, because it is far. We say we can't fly, that we'd like to, to go, but the fingers fly.

Spring

Dear Heinrich,

The practical accomplishment of safe and smooth procurement of this material can be most suitably effected in the form of a directive. A pupil shall be charged with safeguarding the material, and it shall be her job to prepare a series of photographs to establish, insofar as what is humanly recognizable: descent, birthdate, and other vital points. She has proven herself quite capable, though I had my doubts. I said, what is a photograph but a bothersome water stain of what's gone? But she showed me how she works, and this pupil proves the news to her professor, as it were. She is able to procure, from the picture alone, more information than if bodies were before her, or a skull in her lap, though at times I have seen her on the hill by my lab, holding one up, as if catching stars in her skullen basket at night.

Subsequently, when the death has been effected—the head should not be injured!—she severs the heads from the bodies, sending them on, immersed in white buckets filled by a sumptuous material. The photographs, and finally, skulls, will then form my lecture on comparative anatomical research to pre-medical majors at this, the University of Strassburg, all of whom have, I believe, the dream to continue on, and remove bones.

Yours,
August

August Haas walks through Reading alone.

He buys salmon from Su-Yon, from Thai Imperial PAGODA, which is still as there as everything, redlit, even students still, anthropologizing again, everyone. The salmon comes as he's imagined, pink and hotplump, grapefruitgorgeous, the bones almost inconsequential—you could eat them almost, dissipatious in the mouth. $4.50. A dollar more in price equals ten years longer, inflation stifled in the Terminal, in immigrants. This must be Su-Yon, he thinks, a young woman not too young, and thin, the hair all black, no green. He imagines giving her all of his money—not much. The inverse of his debts. I am a student.

He gives her an eight-dollar tip.

"Do you remember Luther? My brother Luther Haas?"

Reckless. He doesn't want his father to see him, who hasn't seen him, who hasn't been. My father for years.

Su-Yon blinks, is prurient, or orient. He never knows what he means, the words that flood studying. "Luther!" She's loud because of Reading. She isn't a loud person. The line is long. Her hands are horrible. Are maroonrimmed and salmonsteamed, the creases burned. Her face is—he isn't looking.

"I knew an Amish kid named Luther Haas, yes, when I first moved here and began working with my aunt, but it's hard to remember what happened in the first year, because I was still learning English and it was difficult. My parents had died, like a fairytale, in a car, and I was dependent on cigarettes my brother would send me from Thailand, which are a little bit sweet, and have cheerful packaging—it was the packaging I enjoyed. I don't remember very much from that year because the whole time I was interacting with anyone, I was thinking about my parents, flashes of their thighs and chins, and about what you might be saying in English and what I was thinking in Thai, and as much as I tried to convince myself to practice, those English words felt like throbbing pieces of wood being whacked on my head for no reason—I couldn't understand learning. I couldn't understand that I would be staying. I wanted to live on the beach with my brother. He was the real next of kin. I didn't understand that he was a drug addict who would soon die in a delirium of seeing something too far away in the ocean, and everyone knew that, could see it coming in, which is why they sent me here, why he went out there, to touch it. I didn't know anything about that, or knew it only in strange places, flashes. I knew it once for an entire second. Horrible, mutated second, while frying salmon, the repetition of frying salmon, so many millionsalmon, delivering me a crystal whack of that horrible thing. And I remember, with Luther, it was relief, we were just two kids having some sex and it wasn't English lessons for either of us. Nobody was a fucking teacher. It wasn't like an education, my coming into an understanding. These flashes we had were just fucking in the car, undressing and wriggling and turning—he used his suspenders once to whip my back. Like a horse. He horsefleshed my ass. He whipped my mouth. In between some kissing. At first, he wanted only to enter my anus, but when we had sex in the correct way, or in the manner I desired, the vagina so much closer to my clitoris, a future seemed more interesting, a future of vaginalfucking, the clitoris implicatious at least, for maybe one minute. I, frying salmon again. I remember he thought my cigarettes were amazing, but they were so incredibly mild, sweetened—I really loved the packaging. But then, my brother sometimes sent a tiny bag of cocaine inside the box, because that was something he would enjoy, and he loved me and thought of me as himself in the way that an egoist loves. A ragamuffin sprite, a narcissist. I couldn't believe how he'd orchestrated this, walking up from the beach and going to the post, to send me something as dear to him as cocaine. The post, the walk from the beach to the post and myself, his moving temple. I always threw this away promptly, the bag, afraid of legalities and my aunt and also of becoming too talkative or egoistic, and the coming down feeling of your skin being erased from the inside by someone so furious with what they've already written, which he'd described to me, joyfully, spitting, but because I loved him and in many ways wanted to be just like him, a true Thai beach bum, I would take my aunt's stuffy old boxes of Knox Gelatin, the kind still came from Bethlehem, before that factory closed down, the still authentic stuff, which they used to make by horse, the bones ground by men, still American, and which my aunt used and still uses, regretting that it will run out at some point and ruin us, ruin our stand, which she uses still to feed our salmonclone from Thailand and the subsequent clones, so that Thai Imperial PAGODA may always prosper, our salmon so strong and light, their uteruses duplicatious, so delicious, like the pinkbeef of a cloud—and the bones nice and thin—you could almost eat them— and I would sprinkle this Knox into my cigarettes before smoking, and it was so nice when I was fifteen and not understanding any English, to feel like my brother a little, a little like a beach bum in Thailand in the middle of Philadelphia and this new way of monotony and too many people I'll never really know—I felt just like him, and I spoke to him in my smoking, our violet telephone. Your brother, Luther Haas, of Haas Family Butter, loved them—he, too, enjoyed them. And I loved that about things. He was like my brother in these moments, us in my aunt's car, smoking on the sand, the honkinggeese streets, the beach above us. Suspenders soft on my buttock, Thai silk, my brother's silkthin rags, his spirit. And the butter he once used on my clit, unsalted, almost white—hard, unforgiving butter he had to melt in his mouth, his heartheated tongue, salmonsliver, pinksilver. I still remember that move. But yes, he did soon stop working here with his father and I remember nothing any longer."

"Can you repeat that!"

She speaks too softly. Her line is long. I shouldn't have made this stupid attempt. This is nothing. Too much. Awg walks out on Arch, in avoidance of the Amish half, Filbertine. And now, in avoidance of Su-Yon forever, embarrassed for apologizing, for what? For asking. For what? A book.

Book of Luther. Sound barrier. I couldn't hear her! Not my brother. I didn't even want to see her. August, it's obvious—where is your sister?

Olivia fucks Adele. It's not fair for it to only go in one direction. Olivia tends to Adele on a Saturday morning. She levers the offer, wrenching her friend from her Synagogue plans. Adele, losing her religion in a room full of moaning. It's easy to wrench her.

"My father killed many creatures, and then he was killed, on the floor of his factory on a Sunday, by an unknown—no one knows. The last time I saw him, he was a mound."

They've put towels down, and scarves, and woolen items. They've put music on—utilitarian, to prevent sound. Olivia slowly uses her fist, small splayed bouquet of bones, the skin warm. She holds one breast, the weight of bread forgetting itself. She holds it patiently, like someone holding something for someone while they moan. Polite and acute, her wrist small, her forearm in. Adele thinks, I am supposed to be chanting, to be sitting and standing, to be angry at Beth, and to be praying. Olivia thinks, this is when I usually use the bathroom, when the entire dormbathroom is mine. The blessed privacy. But sex is like privacy, like a pyre. Olivia moves her hand that is holding Adele's breast to the clitoris, the bloated drip of flesh, the mottled maroonrimmed rags, the mutilated lung of something who swam, the jellyburble, the fishbeef, the flower of guts. This is what Adele wants. Olivia takes out her fist. She uses her rightfingers on it for the heft of an hour, Adele in a tuba languor, but flutelight in her eyewhite! She closes her eyes. When she opens them, the room is small. Olivia is dressed and reading, the braided strings of ten tampons like macramé in her underwear, her fingers squeaking sweet with soap.

"I have to read! I have to finish this by tomorrow!"

"Tomorrow is Sunday, Olivia," Adele gruffs.

"I know! But I have to finish!" Malaise and ease, eagerness viscous with easiness. She's got it. "We meet in the library tomorrow, with the teaching assistant. He insists. Before break."

"Are you sure it's not a trick, just to see you," Adele asks. Her jealousy is actually melodious.

"No, I'm sure, Adele! August Haas has moved on, for sure, to Antigone Edelberg."

"Adele wants to become a doula," Beth sighs to Antigone. "She skips our lectures to go to some class off campus. She comes back sometimes with her hands still filled from going inside women who are birthing, their wombs she says the stretchy caves of heaven. Maroonrimmed, even her arms! Pulling out children. It's disgusting."

Beth enjoys cadavers, vivisection, the wondrous unliving! She talks with Dr. Edelberg over them in the Dreaded Circle after lectures, the other students draining. He tells her how he came to be a surgeon: "I went to London not to finish an education, but to begin one, the beginning of my time with Dr. Elijah Burritt. The life that I would lead as his student—his house was full of animals, their skulls, of the vivisected work of flattened loins, nerves sprawled behind glass pieces, tinged to be seen, and unfeeling: there were three live leopards in his yard.

"They broke free on my first night to eat the dogs. There was howling and bloodshed, and I saw my teacher's ankles knocking together in fear as he locked up his cats. He returned to my bed and told me that one of them should die in the morning. I killed her using a lancet, the other leopards watchful, and I, carrying her, the velvet collapse of killed muscle, to breakfast.

"I, too, was dutiful.

"I had to run her blood into bowls. Burritt lectured, 'Blood is alive,' and he put his hand into the unflagging dissemination of her veins. 'Here,' he said, and I tasted from his finger the cherries soured in liquor, and his finger, a birdstudent and its dropper.

"After this, there were others, several infant elephants arriving already dead—we only wanted from these their skeletons. We chopped through them and finding bone, like finding piping

---

underneath graycountryside, white plumbing of a fled civilization. Dead. You can find anything, see anything, receive anything, drag anything indoors, Beth, put anything on the table, kiss anyone, swallow any amount of blood, different kinds of it, and even, I learned in my first evening in London—the moon risen into a balloon of bedlinens—the white bedblood of men."

Beth tried to understand! "I want to understand everything your father says!" She kneels toward the cocaine, which is missing.

"We can only have a little bit this afternoon," Antigone explains. "I have to finish a book by tomorrow for our library group."

"I thought you weren't going there any longer!" Beth feels desire, the cocaine missing.

"What else does he say?" Antigone asks.

"This isn't a conversation!" Beth feels trapped, like going down to her room. I'll wait for Adele. I'll go to Synagogue again!

"Just stand up and be him. Be him talking at a Quaker meeting." Antigone pours her a line, an offering, for performing. She wants to hear her father through this piece of pippery. Beth, our violet telephone. Beth kneels, devout to it, devout to kneeling, but needing reasons. The cocaine, millionflock of boneproton, floods in, splays spasms in her head. Unfurls the fast unshimmering. Talkative:

"I learned to read all alone. I went to a hill and learned, digesting the wires of every letter, until my learnbrain was wired. I learned and showed my mother, so she wouldn't read out loud to me any longer. I showed her my brain, putting it out on the kitchen table for inspection. I didn't read for her reasons. I didn't read in my room or at the schoolhouse or on the hill to find out what happened. I read to forget. That's it!

"I often found a cabinet. I was indeed in hiding.

"I am trying to remember religion, Beth, before it came to the kitchen, in the formation of those dreadful lessons. About what had happened!

"I remember learning the dreadful lesson in my mother's kitchen about August Hirt, German physician and professor of anatomy at the University of Strassburg. Dr. Hirt, professor and surgeon, experimental on the bodies of the Jews, his sentences—herr editor, experimental murderer, editing out our alphabet. Twisting letters like wire, into numbers. Six million. Numbing no one. Now I am a surgeon. I come in peace, holding out my knife, my sharpflag, my hook, one of four tenaculums, coming in peace with my single skill which I drill in your silk!

"I became a Quaker under the tutelage of Burritt, who had met Fox in London. Burritt advised, Be religious, Edelbergus (we spoke in Latin), but not enormous. Be quiet! And so good it was to meet with him in silence. To be done. To not provoke, or ornament, or remember the terror. We, together, removed it, terror. Only eight, nine cuts, and not with knives."

"My father said this?"

"I'm sure of it!" Beth is not sure. She's stopped taking notes, too rapt is her listening, too shivering are her hands. Quaking and writhing, withdrawing. "I learned of Hirt when I was very young. My mother showed a series of photographs. And it made me so fearful! When she had her left eye extirpated, I wept fearful, so afraid of the doctor hollowing her leg, joyously dipping sharpness into her eye, bucking his knife through her brain. His knife was a mouth and his hand was a stomach, and the doctor's palm was fat because it was heartplumped.

"And then her breast was cancerous, and she had to return to him, and I, young, imagining Hirt using her breast on his mouth, or slicing down her torso and lighting a match near her spine, for fun, the column toppling down. She had her left eye removed, and her left breast, and I hated her doctor—unforgivably a father—and wanted to murder that murderer, experimenting like this on my mother, feeding her horse drugs, ripping her flanks off, sawing out her teeth to use as dice, in a game, to grind down, her bodyparts floating in his refrigerator. Eating her breast with a spoon, spooning it down him, spitting out the nipple like a bone. Terror of being exposed to all of this! Those pictures. The photographs she shoved against my naked two-pupil in the kitchen when I was four, five. Where did she have them from? I waited for her frantically, those three times in that waiting room in Germantown, my heart escaping, wearing itself out on the ceiling, a bloodballoon, with whatever child sitter sitting with me then. There was no other number. I killed my own father.

"And he has bemoaned us, his students . . ."

"How? What does he say about that?"

Beth stands. I was already standing.

"It is I who know what he is doing—you can make your own felicitious decisions. It is I who teach you—look at you looking at me, notetaking, too serious, not ever solicitous, I notice, of one another, who look away from each other as vultures do in the arena a carcass makes of the grass—your hearts are splints only strapped to my table and your eyes are the resurrection of your hearts through your flesh, split and expeditious."

"That sounds like him," Antigone concurs.

There is silence, concurrence.

"I'd offer you more cocaine," Antigone continues, "but I can't."

"Why is that!"

"Your nose—your enormous schnaaaz—is bleeding."

Beth bleeds all Saturday evening, Adele in the room. They both skip dinner, the prayer. The several.

"Did Antigone Edelberg punch you?" Adele kids, annoyed. Annoyed by the blood. Unsexual, sisternal.

"No, she didn't Adele."

"You might as well put a tampon in your nostril. You might as well . . ."

"I bet I know who has one . . ."

"Don't bother Olivia!" Adele pips, a ribbon slipped, her whippingpip, a joycrack.

Heinrich,

I have ordered my pupil to cut up these bodies and have them burned . . . When this work had been finished in the room where the buckets were, I asked her the next day whether she had cut up all the bodies, but she replied: "I couldn't cut up all the bodies, it was too much work. I left some in the bathroom." I then asked her, "And did you burn bodies with their teeth?" At this moment she laughed with a closed mouth, and handed me about a dozen dice, several of which I include in the corners of this packet. And of the bathroom, I went in there and witnessed several bodies draped over one particular toilet, their skin moist with rot, velvetish. Their eyes are reported violet.

Come, oh come and see me,
Your August

August waits in the library for his students, in the morning. He has them meet in the Harold Knox memorial reading room, Shakespearean. Here is a glass case holding Shakespeare's mulberry branch. William. And an oaken splinter from the bedpost whence he was born, his glove in another glasscontainer. And a portrait bright, bottomlit, of Harold Knox, my unliterary father. Small decent room, wooden, green. Not ornate, only old, the goodfeel of wood over, say, metal or steel, a barn over an elevator—I requested it, they meet me here.

He takes out *Lear*, his own annoyed copy, annoyed by his pen, the globular circles, the harassed, etched pages, privatepoems, and in another glasscase, a manuscriptpiece—they must see this! King Lear's death. Here at the University of Pennsylvania, in handwriting. Shakespearean. Not Knoxious.

"I've never been here before," Olivia lies.

"It is hard to find on the third floor here," says August. "Do you have your graphbook?"

Olivia knows how this will go. They will graph all afternoon. She wears eight tampons, a pad, is prepared. "Yes, I brought it."

My students don't appreciate graphing, Awg thinks in disgust. But I had to find books in the trash! The Mennonites, their books. Beyondbibles, several fables. And I graphed these fables onto my barn's thinbrown, using what I had, the stains of worms, flowers elfin, their tonguebraised stamens, grasssmearings and dung, blood and stone I tried grinding, and God gathered these things, my graphings, and left His rainbow, the earth's new architecture, fitting to the overarching heavens, on the thin ceiling, and I arriving, to the

University of Pennsylvania, to study English herein, having already studied everything, knowing everything—that Olivia is bleeding.

Antigone Edelberg is here. Late.

"I hope you will all take a moment, at some point during this hour, to spend some time with the manuscript, which describes, in this instance, Lear's death—please do not look yet if you haven't done your reading. I have colored pencils here on the table—and Antigone, may I please see you after?"

Shameless, Olivia thinks—August Haas. Doesn't know anything. I could menstruate all over this chair and he'd only think I'd cut off my arm. He wouldn't even understand. Maybe I will, here on my father's chair. He died, found on return that evening. From the hospital, the moon bleating the clouds off its farm. The factory to sell. Its pieces, piecemeal, knives and buckets, longtables. And Bethlehem nothing now, the deadtown, murderbroken. Hellsnakes slimmed down, the redworms starving. Too used to blood in Bethlehem.

"Is that Shakespeare?" Antigone asks, bored with graphs, wanting tactility.

"No, that's a portrait Harold Knox, who owned Bethlehem Knox until four years ago, when he was murdered. They made gelatin."

"Thanks Olivia, but let's get back to graphing."

"Who killed him?" Antigone wants to know.

"Please, return to the plot. What do you think are the high points for Lear?"

Olivia can feel herself bleeding, wants to yank out her tampons, eight of them, present them, evidence of something. Of insides. To ruin the library for August Haas, to hang her tampons from a mulberry branch, like bloodlanterns. Warnings. The books to come. By women. To splint him.

His mother had a son, Luther. She had five dead daughters. They did not see doctors.

Her husband, Haas, forgot her. He remembered his son, Luther. He remembered God. He thought of God pushing on his back, pushing him into work. He thought of the hand of God, a giantfinger, hard on his shoulder, a long fleshbird—perched there. He didn't fuck her.

His wife appeared gravid, her front thick with planet. But not from him. She had unlocked the case at the schoolhouse and put its shaggy globe with the continents molted off in her mouth. She had not chewed as it entered her stomach. She was a snake. They named him August, after one of the months, and Dutch, Ow-Goose-tz, and he said to her: "You are selective with their genders. You kill daughters." And he went back to working, holding God as he worked with his scythe, hacking her.

He knew it, Ow-Goose-tz Knoxious. He should be burned like the horses that everyone knew were being burned. Ovencleaned from this continent. How could you not? You knew that. All you had to do was think—look at the smoke streaming from the steel bell and know. Or feel your own cough. His real son, Luther, went with him to Reading. August, stay home. Don't show him to books. Let him be in the barn alone. Don't let him work. Don't let him feed God.

Awg killed flowers all over his body. His fingers swelled to kill. And stones were stars, fallen and found again. By me! He dragged them over the lungs of flowers, killing them. And God saw what he did and tore out His eyes, and here are all of my stars. And I was called by my mother, seventeen. From my barn. To be called is to be unheard. Unfound.

She buggytook him, him driving, them to Bethlehem.

She showed him her workstation in the long kitchen. He was fragile in watching what she did. Her heart was still a milk, a blood of sugarbird. You would drink its blood directly if she leant it down and opened herself with a knife. You would almost use a knife yourself. Instead, he worked. She showed him how to work there, where the buckets were of powder. He worked because his mother was watching. Her eyes were everything. I don't have her heart any longer, her eyes are her heart, split. I don't have her hands, her eyes are her hands. I don't have her breasts, her eyes are two of them. I never had my father, I, existing.

And then he saw him, carrying a shortknife and long hose.

Knox said, "Good, you've brought me some help." His face was hooded by Awg's unlooking. Largesized, a bison. You could feel him. "We'll start you as a hoseman."

They had to walk outside.

A sunset is an orange bison disintegrating. With ripe red horns. The bright bull is being slaughtered on a brass floor.

They went inside again, in the new room, tongue-ripped innard of a heavy black bell, where it was done, the horses slouched and cut in death, boneripped. Their dilapidated skin. Faces long. Blood ankling. "Alright August," said his father, herr employer, "wash the floor."

He deboned him. He used tools, the ones locked in the case, his elbow perforatious on glass to release use. It wasn't difficult. It was ease, a long knife floating in. He moved around the heart as he cut as if cutting to remove it, eightcuts, but not that. I don't want it. He removed the bone, drawing upward white prizes—I could have used these. Used everything. Ribs, a winter sled. Shoulder blade, my flute. Everything. Skin, my blanket at night. Hair, stuffed into a cushion. Stomachlining, waterbucket. Sinews, my first bow. Horn, my spoon. Don't leave anything in the ankling. Heartglue! The horses, he saw, were wearing diapers on their hooves—he knew of it, the diaper cure for molting feet, a myth, ridiculous, forced to trod inside acrylic meant for the excrement of the innocent, as if this would cure them from disease, which was this, Knox—their disease of becoming what would become of them. He washed them.

Beth is saying goodbye to Antigone, is buying cocaine. For cocaine, she's performing Dr. Edelberg again:

"My mother showed me those pictures of Dr. Hirt and his skulls lined in rows at the kitchen table, on that thing, Shabbat, and I wanting to burn them with our two-candle, the twinflame, feed them, our burning pet who could hotmouth this undinnerous filth, its two-teeth grinding photography to gray flour. I wanted to grab them from her, these pictures of perhaps my father—a skeleton swooned in Herr Surgeon's arm, him shaving flesh, almost just rubbing it off—and I'd feed them to Shabbat. Shabbat! Shabbat! Come here, boy, eat this, but it was late, they, image, image, passing into my young-eye and pouring into the cushion . . .

"In this one, pointing to a heart, having popped it out its person, oiling. Pinkoiling. Redoil. The body crooked and lewd, hips like sharp ship tops. 'This is what happened, Son,' she said. To me! To whom? 'This is Holocaust education,' she explained, schoolhousing the kitchen. Wallpapering the table, fallen wall, in grayswirls of skullish horror, All the graywater, the flesh a slop in the sink in the back. I couldn't wash a dish. Eat!

"It was violence! It stayed moving in a circle in the ball. She showed me a Diary. She wanted me to learn it. She'd read it out loud, she said, by the side of my bed, if I wouldn't learn yet. 'Can't you read?' I tried. They weren't words, weren't the animals of my mouth, whom I freed and freed and freed. I couldn't read."

Beth sits. Quiets.

"Antigone, are you going home for break?"

"No, no. My father is working, many surgeries. And Quakers don't go bonkers over Easter. It's not like that, I'll just study."

"Ok, Adele is waiting. Take care!" She puts cocaine, well earned, in her wool, checked and dull. It brightens my hand. "Wait. But what about your mother? Is your mother home?"

"My mother is in an insane asylum. Wait—I do have one more question."

"Ask me!" Beth pips, generous. Doesn't want to go down to Adele, to the first floor, and to seder, their mother ill, uncooking for them, laying down, in her bed drowning. My mother's mattress the torn boat. A person a boat, too, who rips, water whipping you, coming through you, the sun nothing, not an island. They'd bring a plate to her. Undivotous. Nondevoted. Whatever. "Seriously. I'm sorry your mother's not well. Ask me anything—anything you want to know."

"My drugdealer wants the last name of Olivia, your sister's girlfriend."

Beth, furious. She runs down the stairs. She bursts in. Bloodankled from the hall, the blood flooding, "I'm not going!"

Beth,

It has been harrowing. The seder went fine. You were not here to ask the fourquestions and no one is younger than you. Mom in her bed— Mom asking about you. She is wearing a diaper now, the bathroom too far. It is harrowing to change it—I'm changing majors. I don't want to be premedical any longer. I don't want to think about blood or shit, the brownrobbins burnt dead, the deadplums, any of it, or bones and lungs—your Edelbergian things. No longer. I want to do something more general.

And where are you living now anyway? Hasn't the first floor been evacuated due to flooding? Don't they need to deepclean the carpets of blooding? Where have you ascended to anyway, Beth, or what ark do you take? What tack? Where can I find you when I return? Better to have come home with me on the train—gin rummy, maybe—and let them clean—I can't imagine where you'll stay.

And Beth, Olivia Knox is Not my girlfriend.

Adele

Antigone takes the elevator. The dorm is clear, clean of people. Gentle without them. She takes the elevator to August's room. Strange to live here as a senior. He rooms alone on a quiet floor, with other strangepeople, nonfreshmen. She needs more cocaine. There are shushing signs on the walls and the hush of a holiday anyway. She could scream or do anything, any sound. She can't think of one.

He sold it, the gelatin, brought down in its bucket, the bucket between his knees on the bus, suspenders off—not Amish. He put it in smallbags the kind he'd seen Luther bring in the barn, sniffing and declaring, "No, it isn't the same, not Su-Yon's." His brother coming in with these bags from Reading, small and soft, part pillow, for a specimen, pouring them, winding lines of grain, barnlanes, on the barefloor, wooden, sniffing them. Trying so hard to smell something. He watched his brother dying—he'll die, Awg thought, of talking. Of smiling like that, teeth a moonbracelet screwed behind his lips. Their dark backs. Thinner, the suspenders doing more literal work in holding up his brother, the pants, mothersewn. Barnruiner.

You, ruin us.

Awg once a visitor. He was home this latest summer. Before our fall semester. Only for you, Luther. To see you in the barn. Living. I thought I had left forever, on my bus to Glen Park, a Quaker area south of here—here, Luther, were fieldsquares fenced and even, the land wending and holding onto nothing. Where are the cows? Where are the horses and barns? Green and pleasing, horizonline the longwhip of greenribbon, grass short here as fizzing. Maintained hills, nonmountainous. Houses large, almost mansionous, farmshaggy and fancy, a froth of shutters and planters, a paint, a kind of crust.

In the park, I slept. I hid my bucket in a bush and slept on a bench.

The children of doctors want powders, Luther. They want it dressed in a bag and bought for a lot. They don't care what! I was selling the bucket into bags increasing in size, some the floppen heft of rabbits, the kind you'd kill, Luther or, I've seen you, fetal, pulling. I slept in an empty field, worms salivating for dung, and you could fling them. I flung them at the sun, brightisland, from my greenboat, my darkgreenboat, my blackeningboat, my big empty deck, hillwobbling, stillfloating—where going? I checked the trash for books, the better reading, more egalitarian, of the Quaker people—beyondbibles in the rubble, finding Russians—Natasha on her windowsill before she found religion, before religion wasn't stargazing—and writings from William Penn, founder of this land, to and about his friend, to Fox, the George of Glen Park's bench. A plaque told me this much.

My Kind Friend, George Fox,

If a door is in your way, break it like a mirror and come here. If the door is violet, shoot it.

That you too could taste the peaches growing inherent in here, rotting into white wine-syrups, and see here these fish and those fowl, the soil . . . blackcrying with richness, which the peaches ingest. I have this house.

Let me describe it.

I. The land containeth diverse kinds of earth, as yellow and black, poor and rich. I have seen more blackness in it than the heavens, and worms—many molten fingers of purple nightgowns, I find them everywhere!

II. The air is sweet, heavens serene, like the south-parts of France (we have been), and rarely Overcast.

III. The natural produce of the country, of vegetables: trees, fruits, plants, flowers. The trees are the black walnut, cedar, cypress, chestnut, poplar, gumwood, hickory, sassafrax, ash, beech and oak: of all which there is plenty for use.

IV. The natives are tall, straight, well built, needing no protection from the sun. The flattened nose, so frequent with blacks, is not common to the natives, and I am ready to believe them of the Jewish Race for these reasons: I find them of like countenance and their children of so lively Resemblance, their noses like mangled fins seeming torn from ancient sharks, even right after birth. But this is not all—they mourn for one year, like the Jews, and there are the similar customs of their women—these naked nativewomen going out after bleeding, the monthly feminine condition, to plunge into my pond.

Your Kind Friend,
William Penn

On the Character of George Fox, Preeminent Quaker of London

I.   God endued him with clear and wonderful depth.

II. But above all, he excelled in prayer. The most awful, living and reverent frame I ever felt was to approach him in his praying. We had come from my pond, and I began to brew a fire against its backdrop of brick, giving the logs shoves, showing him my spirit about it, but turn'd and saw him praying. I sat and watched as one sits on a roof's rim and opens his entire brain.

III. He was of an innocent life, no busybody nor self-seeker, neither touchy nor critical: what fell from him was very inoffensive. I took him to the park and lifted what he praised as asphodel. He sat on the bench and was Silence, no doubt recalling the sheep of his farm in a Leicester youth. I saw that he began to name or recall their names, and shower his mind through their living wool. I mentioned to him the animals indigenous here, of fish and fowl, the plentiful horses broken out across our hill—and our tree-kinds—and he looked up from his bench baggy-lipped as was his happiness, from as if a mist of sheep and spoke almost raggedly through their fog.

IV. He, an incessant laborer.

V.   "What is this?" Fox asked. The Native women in their Jew-like bathing had filled the pond for our use. It smelled. Of oiled steel. I put my foot in, taking off a big boot, my planter's boot. It came up a murky orange, and when dipping in my calf, my calf was yellow, the water a molten parrotbutter of the parrots I have seen. Not in this country. I jumped. The pond was thick to move myself through, though I did squirm the oiled steel, and was naked, my white and brown clothes, leather and wool, heaped as facetious mushrooms on the grass, and I beckoned to him. "But what is this?" he was blurting, his fingers tremulous as fawnspines on his bootstraps. "Come in!" I beckoned, and to show further what this was, I put my head in, coming up green and orange-soaked, red, and I smiled so happily then, my chest churning parrotparts. "Come in!" I called to him. He did. He disrobed, all his buckles and wrappings, and came in. Leaving England.

I joyously kissed him. My lips drip'd with blood. His nose was a woolen green. He turned, initiating my being behind. The oil still squirmed. His lips blooddripped. I ate blood off his tongue like a person who eats paint. Like someone insanity has given flowers. I blew him, on the bank, his violetcock coming, me still in the water, mermaidous, murmen, menial—I, working. Putting my tongue to his tendril, to his fawnspine responding, to a purplereach, who reached for me. I made him come, my body silly in the water still. I swallowed what I could, the serum too filling, come all the way from London.

We left our clothes heaped so not to ruin them by our fingers and walked back through the fence and my field into the house where I lay'd for us an old sheet, so that we might sit without staining my floor by the fire. My wife wasn't there. She, lying in somewhere. I hoped she'd lie forever! He'll never leave, I imagined. "Don't go back to London," I said. "There are hospitals here." I hung our sheet in the morning like a flag of our fucking. Because I fucked him. Right on the front of my door, here. Fuck everyone. Before going in. Here in the house of Penn. I went to him in the morning but he had bathed, clothed, gone, I should have guessed, to pick his clothes back, the overgrown mushrooms by the morningpublished bank. He was praying now against th'bed, his elbows sharp in the sheet. He was—of course— silent. "Fox . . ." I was whispering, and we walked to the park, and he sat on his bench, and I stood. He told me he was leaving, his lips baggy, eager. I died inside and stood forever.

"Ow-Goose-tz, want this?" my brother was asking. No, I don't want that, but to climb into a cow and fly forever through beefwater.

"No, Luther, I don't want that. And who is that?"

"This is a statue and I'm fuckmelting it into this bucket to sell. You and I will go there tonight, to the factory in your car. You have one, now? You're a student?"

He had in his hand a candle for melting.

"Yes, I will be a senior this fall at the University of Pennsylvania. But Luther—"

"Help me melt him, Awg. If they don't know it's him, they'll take him. We'll sell."

A Haas Family Butter bucket, buttergutted and cleaned out, and the man made to stand inside. Humiliated person. Luther holding the candle, now lit, to its obvious erection. Not a sword, more a scroll. Some kind of dictum.

"Luther, where did you get this?" Awg having seen the other one, the twin, on top of City Hall, what he could see sometimes from his dorm, the dark erection in the sun.

"Why won't he have his meltdown!" The statue resilient. A resilient erection.

"Where did you get him?" August asking.

"In Glen Park. A man was watching me. He said, 'Take him. Take the one who is standing.' I asked if it was gold and he laughed at me. He asked if I was Amish and I said 'No,' and he, 'Then where are you going?' and I, 'Not home,' and he, 'Then where?' and I, 'Where I—' and he, 'In here?' and I, 'Here in . . . ?' and he, 'I am—' and I, enterous, his house, and he, 'I, Dr. Edelberg,' and I, 'Luther,' and he,

'I am blind' and I, 'And how did you think then that I was Amish?' and he, 'I heard the panting of a horse on your breath, the buggy that waits for you in your throat like a curved road at midnight,' and I told him how I had wanted to find some metal to sell, for cocaine, that I had come down this road for scraps, and that I would kill horses! The ones waiting in my throat. I'd swallow so hard.

"He showed me Venus, a planet, through a tube. Knowing where his things are. Not blind at all. And then he hugged me touching my cheeksilk and I touched his nose and it was as hard as the dead, their elbowhard blood. He showed me his study, where there are many maps of the body. He let me search through his books for all the parts. The anus is what you call this. The anus. And the heart escapes us. In surgery, it can be cut out and it escapes, humorous. Isn't it interesting, August? He made me read aloud to him. 'Here's my hand,' I read. 'Touching you. Here. Now follow me,' I said. We stood in his study, his daughter asleeping, and a surgeon he was, of the University of Pennsylvania hospital west of Reading. He, explaining. He has removed many organs, Awg, and he told me how, and how he used them all, fuckopening people, taking things out of them all of the time, that you can remove anything as long as they are asleeping, but I stopped his lips with my fingers that so suddenly flew to him like birds given drugs, or motives, and told him, 'Love is insertion.'"

Luther was sniffing more from his palm. Now gentle. Like a calf. Morning growing a fog of canaries, dogged into parrots in the trees. They could see through the barn, the barn thin.

"We had to walk to the park, because of his daughter asleep. Tomorrow beginning to attend the University of Pennsylvania as a freshman. 'To study what,' I asked to be politeness, my anus pulsing, and he, 'Nothing, not doctoring. I'll probably not see her again.' Morning was coming. A fleet of pinkflowers staining and stinging the clouds, that flew dying. The flowerlight light between us, still in such blackness, August, but edges soaped with light. My lip out of time, a gone evening, the jellied spine of sunset, and you press it onto another wet, lost piece of it . . .

"Then why are you home? Why didn't you stay with this man?"

"He was dutiful in taking his daughter down to the University of Pennsylvania this morning. And I was a son. And his lover, and Awg, am not Amish anymore but a Quaker . . ."

And Penn still hard, his elbowanxious blood. Gold.

And Antigone, broken.

"I'm not sure what I can do for you then," August is saying in his dorm's doorway, what drug dealers say: I need the money. He comforts himself, it's not a drug, just gelatin—a horse's coffin. What does it even do in anyone? Causing floating? Does their meat float in them, or bones made like shanks of, what, cotton, the skull clouding?

"What are you, not going anywhere for spring break?"

"Oh no—work to do, work to do." Talk like tapping. "I'm grading your plotgraphs, remember? I am a teaching assistant here in my senior year at the University of Pennsylvania. What are you going to do?"

"I'm going to give you a blowjob in the Dreaded Circle on my father's operating table."

Beth finds Olivia in their dorm room—Adele gone. Olivia is smoking. A towel under the door and the window slightly open and no blood to be seen, men cleaning.

"You're not supposed to be here," she sighs, but even her sigh is high, is a flimsy cloak over eagerness bright.

"You mean this isn't my room," Olivia clarifies, "or do you mean because they are evacuating the entire building?"

"Both but everything! This isn't your room and the building is full of your blood, Olivia, a burst pipe they think, and the carpets need cleaning and they're probably going to strip up the carpet but first they want to try shampooing, because they have these machines, but we got all this in a letter, remember, in our mailboxes, official, before they, too, were filled? We have to evacuate! For all of seder."

There was a smell in the hall. Dead plumrobbins.

"I thought you weren't celebrating seder."

"I'm not celebrating seder!" Beth sits down on the floor, bedscared. Olivia isn't dressed, is naked and dry besides a few patches of come like gownfog on her inner thighs, is reading. "This dormroom, Olivia, is no smoking."

Olivia doesn't put her cigarette out. It's so violet. It hardly is one! Something sweet and light you buy on the street in Thai lettering—she enjoys the packaging. The color between her fingers, like a branch of a different ilk on a beech tree, bleached, see, the violet so shocking. She likes to think and smoke. A book is but a prop.

"What are you reading?"

"Oh, something of Adele's." The hebrew letters, I mezuzah-pulled the fetal scroll, their inexplicable architecture. An excuse for drifting. Is all. The cigarette is all, the style. She doesn't inhale, hates smoke. The exhalation of an incinerated horse! "And besides, Beth, you know there's no detector on this floor. Because of all your candles."

"They aren't my candles any longer!" Beth bursts.

To fuck this younger sister is better. Is less vaginal. More mutual. There's more face to kiss. Beth's face isn't large, but more various. Flickerous. Olivia watches her cigarette swimming, violet eeling, in her eyewhite, a crystal that keeps resmashing itself across a pearlwall, and puts it out, the eye, by closing it, and the cigarette still is lit. She puts it out, the cigarette, through Adele's extralong causing an ash-rimmed hole and fucks Beth with the butt in her palm, magic bean in my fist, humming a Hebrew tune for fun. Not knowing one. The trees reach for us, put forth their tender leaves of hope, branches bent and gnawing on the dormwindowpane, hoping, too, to get in.

I said I would free them. My feet collected weepscratchings from the grass, barefoot, my diaper on—could not bear to buy tampons, the WaWa awash in too much fluorescence, I was nauseous. Diaperous. I went out to our factory to free them at night. That night. Free them up the hills from which we'd scalped them. Bethlehem. I'd lead them from their steel enclosure in my nightgown, whatever.

But he was there. In the center. On the floor. Horseflesh rumpled around him. Clean, someone had cleaned them, their coats crackling with eyewhite. I freed others, younger ones in the other rooms. You can't shoo a horse. You have to work. I led them. And I reigned the stubborn ones and I pulled them. In the field they terrified deer, who fled, and they, following.

"I have some cocaine for us," Beth delights. She pours her bag out obscuring Hebrew letters, that clatter of banisters, and Olivia marveling, laughing, almost gruff—"You think that's cocaine, Beth? It's Knox." Lighting another sweet violet. "You get high on this stuff? It's gelatin. It's horse au gratin!"

August watches for Antigone's mouth in the dark, which stretches gray. The moon is in the window above them, seen, white spotlight, faint. Her mouth, a mauve serum in the room.

Antigone needs more cocaine, so will sell her serum, and tongue, in vials, however, however vile, in order to float again, the heart ballooned, empty and rising. She can feel her heart dropping, choking with earth.

"I can't tell if you want this, Antigone, if you're just doing this for cocaine—and that's not a good feeling."

He feels Amish again, a Haasish person, or Hasidim, bartering, the lovebarters of religion, drugdealing.

"That's asking a lot from me right now. I'm still grieving my dead boyfriend, remember?"

"How did he die again?"

"That I can't say." He didn't die. Beth found him. As promised. She found Penn. She pointed right to him from the windowpane, from floor 7. Not a sword or scroll, only his hand extending. Dark erection seeming, the sun behind him. He'd risen. "Take these down."

Penn had not needed such direction, had been dressed, undressed, simultaneous. And William's cock would not have slumped in my mouth, slumberous across the jaw, an ill manatee needing reminding, tonguebullying, so that a vein finally begins, bellies, deadhardening on the underside of this sluglog, amphibious warthoggery, no, thin, this worm I want to be flinging.

They climb from the dormwindow, the building bleeding.

Beth pushes the window up farther, a winter that crackles with a static of spring, leaves still small, still scrolled, fruition coming, a greenfruit, flat—not long. The stillwinter air crackling with something not warm, a cold messenger of warmletters, still unopened. I'll read them to you.

It's not far to the ground. This is the first floor of the dormbuilding of the University of Pennsylvania. The blood had begun to collude, lanes of it bellyspreading into puddles the carpet drank making dark. The smell of roasted birds, of plumserum burning. They could hear the elevator filling, buttons lit red, maroonrimmed and dripping—out of order. They wondered if the men, who were here for cleaning, were drowning. I won't help them!

Olivia, dressing, putting regular things, pants, her shirt and pea coat, regulations, over gownstains. They don't need to jump because a branch extends, has always been, extending to them, branch-in-waiting, winter's sassafrax, the only one on campus among beech and elm and oak—a tree known for its joints.

On the branch:

"The factory is gone. They took it down. They melted its metal rim, selling the melt for steel. The horses were found across the crust of forest, dead of starvation, of seizures and memories. No one ate them.

"Let's get off this branch, I feel it swaying too much. Sassafrax, Beth, is not known for its strength."

In the Dreaded Circle, Dr. Edelberg's last lecture for the semester at the University of Pennsylvania is on Womb Duplicatum. Spring is human.

Beth sits alone.

"Separate them.

"Womb Duplicatum, a subject in which I had experimented with my master. Together we had taken a second womb out of a woman. It had been bleeding her to death. We kept it in a jar on the table as do others with a vase of flowers. This was our honest way, and I had requested of my friend that he let me saw it open, but Burritt would not allow it. 'There are barriers,' he lectured, among his opened elephants and parted skulls, so it remained, bag full of anything, fog, unknown balloon, bobbing in a serum of gelatin sent here from Bethlehem, in the center of our table, in London. And here again, a woman has been given to the University of Pennsylvania, with a case of Womb Duplicatum, but more urgent as her bleeding is external—I understand your dorm rooms fill. I remember this procedure well. It must be done quickly! Students, we will separate these—one grips the other—using a hook with a shoulder.

"Listen to my thinking.

"The womb I want is behind the one we must leave in. It is deeply behind. I have taken out eyes, cut away whole tumor-heavied breasts, lifted off people's feet, calves, up to their thighs, and have made eight cuts and collected the heart—out—have dove in my knifesuit to come down for half the liver, excised the penis but never once have been, without Burritt by my side, alone upon the womb."

Dr. Edelberg sets down his hook with a shoulder. His hands are soft floating forks, fingertine. He removes the womb. Smaller than one bean, butt of cigarette, if it is violet. Remove it.

"We can now dissect this for our use, so we all may note the innerworking. And what is a brain but a moon? But the moon that lights what at night, the heart? You forget to watch! And the heart, the moon is in morning. Who will come down?"

The other students are adjusting their pencils now, a young wood of trees creaking to be tilted and applied. Leafless, stripped for use. They forget to watch! They treat their eyes like bad pupils and whip them with pencils.

Beth only watches. She watches through the woods and past the flux of echoing. Dr. Edelberg beginning incision. It blinds him. She writes it down: What is a rainbow but the colorlegs of light? But a thing off of land, the ground's blown dream, and taut with return . . . and Olivia, living. And Beth is leaving, her name going home.

To Bethlehem.

Acknowledgment

To all of UPenn's readers. From the Missoula novel crew: Aaron Shulman, Anne Marie Wirth Cauchon, Lauren Hamlin, Beth McHugh, and Jen Gann. Thank you Dierdre McNamer, Lisa Schumaier, Brandon Shimoda, Elisabeth Benjamin, Melanie Rae Thon, and Lance Olsen.

Thank you, Trey Sager. You delivered this to me with your readings, your erasures, your listening intelligence, and our walk thru the flowers.

For vital support, thank you to the MacDowell Colony, the University of Montana, the University of Utah, Jacqueline Osherow and the Taft-Nicholson Center, and Casa Westbury.

Also thank you to the rare books librarians and staff at the Marriott Library, the Library of Congress, Pennsylvania Hospital Medical Library, and the Historical Medical Library of the College of Physicians of Philadelphia.

And, thank you, Noemi.

A shout of love to my grandmother, Ruth Kooperman. And for being beyond the reading, thank you, Kristen. Thank you, *Peter.*